S0-BBP-035

"I need to be challenged," Ashley blurted

Luc's eyes became hooded. "You don't think playing a part in a feature film would challenge you?"

"Frankly, no." She lifted her chin defiantly. "I'm a theater person. I'm serious about my profession."

He threw the script on the desk. "You're also the most arrogant, conceited little bore I've ever met. Serious! Do you know what an opportunity you're turning down? Believe me," he grated, "your attitude is that of a rank amateur. You have the gall to think you're too good for the movies. Don't say another thing," he ordered, as Ashley tried to interrupt. "Just get out and stop wasting my time."

He flung open the door, and Ashley, inwardly quaking, folded her coat over her arm and walked out.

Books by Celia Scott

HARLEQUIN ROMANCES
2568—SEEDS OF APRIL
2638—STARFIRE

These books may be available at your local bookseller.

For a list of all titles currently available,
send your name and address to:

Harlequin Reader Service
P.O. Box 52040, Phoenix, AZ 85072-2040
Canadian address: P.O. Box 2800, Postal Station A,
5170 Yonge St., Willowdale, Ont. M2N 5T5

Starfire

Celia Scott

Harlequin Books

TORONTO • NEW YORK • LONDON
AMSTERDAM • PARIS • SYDNEY • HAMBURG
STOCKHOLM • ATHENS • TOKYO • MILAN

Original hardcover edition published in 1984
by Mills & Boon Limited

ISBN 0-373-02638-2

Harlequin Romance first edition August 1984

Copyright © 1984 by Celia Scott.
Philippine copyright 1984. Australian copyright 1984.
Cover illustration copyright © 1984 by Will Davies.

All rights reserved. Except for use in any review, the reproduction or utilization
of this work in whole or in part in any form by any electronic, mechanical
or other means, now known or hereafter invented, including xerography,
photocopying and recording, or in any information storage or retrieval system,
is forbidden without the permission of the publisher, Harlequin Enterprises
Limited, 225 Duncan Mill Road, Don Mills, Ontario, Canada M3B 3K9. All the
characters in this book have no existence outside the imagination of the
author and have no relation whatsoever to anyone bearing the same name
or names. They are not even distantly inspired by any individual known
or unknown to the author, and all the incidents are pure invention.

The Harlequin trademarks, consisting of the words HARLEQUIN ROMANCE
and the portrayal of a Harlequin, are trademarks of Harlequin Enterprises
Limited; the portrayal of a Harlequin is registered in the United States Patent
and Trademark Office and in the Canada Trade Marks Office.

Printed in U.S.A.

CHAPTER ONE

ASHLEY pinned the pear-shaped pearl ornament secure-
ly so that it fell into the centre parting of blonde hair
framing her face. She settled the starched ruff more
comfortably round her throat and pulled her heavily
embroidered stomacher down hard, so that the upward
thrust of her breasts was more pronounced. Satisfied,
she headed for the door, where she turned with an
exclamation of annoyance and came back into the room.

'Damn! I nearly forgot.' She unearthed a pair of
khaki-coloured knee-pads from beneath a tumble of
clothes and pulling up her voluminous damask skirt fixed
the clumsy pads to her rounded knees.

'Ashley, what on earth—!' exclaimed one of her
dressing-room companions, the stick of Leichner stage
make-up poised halfway to her face.

'It's because of all that falling to my knees begging for
mercy in Act three,' Ashley explained. 'Look—bruises
the size of grapefruit!' She pointed dramatically to her
shapely legs. 'This was the costume department's idea.
You'll never know I'm wearing these things . . . not
under all this gear.' She readjusted the full skirt of her
Elizabethan costume and executed an experimental jig.
'There! Secure as the Houses of Parliament.'

'Till they drop to your ankles,' said a thin girl called
Ann who was the third occupant in the dressing-room of
the Royal Theatre. 'Do you want to look ridiculous,
Ashley? Particularly since we've got celebrities in
tonight.'

Ashley recognised the edge to this remark. She was
well aware that Ann found it galling that after three
years' professional experience she was playing a walk-
on, while Ashley, twenty years old and just out of drama
school, had landed a small but showy part in the histori-
cal drama *Elizabeth the Queen*.

5

'Celebrities? What celebrities?' asked Ashley, her curiosity aroused.

Jenny, the third member of the dressing-room, applied eyeliner carefully while she answered. 'Apparently Lucas Martineaux the film director's in tonight looking for talent. Ann's all of a twitter,' she added mischievously, 'she wants to be discovered.'

'By a *film director*!' Ashley was incredulous. 'You don't want to act in films, do you, Ann?'

'You bet I do!' Ann pulled the red wig she wore in the play on to her head. 'Lots of lovely money and a bit of genuine recognition. Beats standing on stage night after night with a gaggle of ladies-in-waiting.'

'I can see your role in this play isn't much fun,' Ashley agreed tactfully, 'but it's not bad enough to make you want to go into *films*, surely?'

Ann's jaw dropped.

'You make it sound like a fate worse than death,' said Jenny, smiling.

'Well, I think it is.' Ashley was filled with youthful fervour. 'I think the stage is . . . is real acting. And films are too . . . too easy. Thoroughly unsatisfying, I should think.'

'And the money you earn making films? I suppose you think that's unsatisfying too?' enquired Ann sourly.

'*Money!*' Ashley's beautifully modulated voice was filled with scorn. 'If money's your only reason for being an actress you might as well marry for it. Why not just look for a rich husband and be done with it?'

The P.A. system suddenly boomed—'Act one beginners, please'—cutting short Ann's indignant reply. Jenny gave a howl of anguish and started pulling on her costume at breakneck speed, while Ann began festooning herself with large paste jewels, swearing volubly all the time.

Ashley left them to it and climbed up to stage level to watch the beginning of the play from the wings. This production had been running for six months, and since this was the last week of the run Ashley didn't want to miss a single moment of the magic being in a hit play held for her. She knew she could never get tired of listening to the excited buzz of the audience before the curtain rose, nor grow blasé to the hush that swept the theatre like a wave when the house lights dimmed. The others could stay in the pokey little dressing-room and gossip if they chose, but that was not for her.

She stood in the wings close to the prop table, which was heaped with gilt-painted goblets and papier-maché food for the banquet scene. It all looked clumsy and unreal at close range, but was utterly authentic and realistic from the other side of the footlights. She watched the curtain rise up into the shadowy flies above her head and listened eagerly to the round of applause that greeted the set. This production starred one of England's most famous theatrical couples, and each time Ashley watched them in their opening scene, skilfully setting the mood for the rest of the act, she felt she was getting a free drama lesson, and one that was just as valuable as the three years' intense studies she'd just completed six months ago.

Her grey eyes lingered on the brightly lit slice of stage beyond the heavy velvet 'teasers' that blocked the back-stage from the audience, and an image of Lucas Martineaux the film director sitting in that vast auditorium floated idly into her head. She hadn't the faintest idea what he looked like—fat, short and middle-aged, probably. This was her image of all film executives. She realised that she had sounded supercilious when she had scornfully dismissed the idea of acting in films to Ann. She had a bad habit of exaggerating and speaking her mind without thinking first; a habit she had spent most of her twenty years trying to curb, without much success. She was absolutely sincere in her attitude to the cinema. Her passion for acting simply didn't include acting in front of a camera. She not only had no desire to appear in television or movies, she harboured a mild contempt for both media. She was honest enough to realise this contempt was based on ignorance, and usually she managed to keep her prejudice to herself.

She noticed that the first of the actors playing courtiers

had made their entrance on to the stage and she put all
thoughts of films versus stage aside and started to men-
tally prepare for her own entrance.

As usual, for Ashley, the three acts flew by. Her big
dramatic scene, the one which required the knee-pads,
since she had to fling herself at the Queen's feet, earned
her a round of applause on her exit, so she was feeling
very pleased with life when she sat down to remove her
make-up after the final curtain-call. Ann didn't share her
mood. She was upset that so far there had been no word
that Lucas Martineaux was waiting backstage anxious to
sign some lucky actress to a five-year film contract.

'He probably left after Act One,' Ann said morosely.
'That means he'll have missed my only little bit of action.
He won't even have noticed me if he didn't see Act
Three.'

Ashley removed her blonde wig and released her own
auburn hair which fell to her shoulders in a glitter of
tousled curls. She fastened it back with a strip of towelling and rubbed cold cream over her face.

'Why don't you ferret him out at his studio or
wherever he hides?' she suggested. 'Beard the lion in
his den.'

'Because he works in North America and I don't have
the fare,' Ann snapped back.' For God's sake, Ashley,
don't you know anything?'

'Not about films. Sorry!' Ashley pulled a wry face at
her glowering colleague and started to dress. The trans-
formation from a demure sixteenth-century court lady to
a stunning twentieth-century girl was quite startling.
And it was more than the blue jeans and canary yellow
sweater that created the contrast. Ashley glowed with
energy. And she was beautiful. Of medium height and
small-boned, she was blessed with a heart-shaped face
and a complexion so fine and creamy it seemed transpa-
rent. Her wealth of curling hair was as lustrous as glass,
and changed colour in the reflection of the light—now
dark chestnut, now burnished copper. Her eyes were
large and almond-shaped with well defined lids, like the
eyelids on medieval carvings, and the eyes themselves

were grey as smoke, except when she was in the grip of an emotion, when they became green and enormous. There was a delicate dusting of pale gold freckles on her straight nose. These were her despair, and at age twelve she had tried to remove them with laundry blueing. Her upper lip was childishly short and appealing. Her lower one curved sensually, and the corner of her mouth dimpled when she smiled. Her chin was round—and stubborn—and her face was a mirror for every emotion she experienced. She could no more control the blushes that swept unbidden to her face than she could control the weather. She was warm, generous, quixotic, and had the devil's own temper.

That she had chosen to become an actress was no surprise to her family. Their only concern was that she would develop a certain toughness in order to deal with such a gruelling profession. At the moment she had no defences, and was as vulnerable as a kitten.

She ran her slender fingers through her unruly locks and zipped up her short bomber jacket.

''Night, girls!' She slung her bag jauntily over her shoulder.

'Don't you want to come for a drink, Ashley?' Jenny asked.

She refused, pleading fatigue. Actually she found drinking with the cast night after night rather boring. They discussed nothing but the theatre and them-selves—a hazard among actors—and while Ashley was enthusiastic about her chosen profession she was also interested in other things. She had discovered that a couple of evenings socialising with her peers was enough in a working week.

She ran up the long flight of stairs to the stage-door exit. ''Night, Bob!' she sang out to the stage-doorman, her clear voice ringing like a bell in the post performance quiet, 'see you tomorrow!'

'Just a minute, Miss Morrison,' the old man waved a piece of paper. 'Gentleman left this for you.'

'For me?' Mystified, she took it. It was the theatre programme folded in two. Opening it up, she found a business card pinned to the inside. Plainly engraved, it read simply, 'Lucas Martineaux . . . Los Angeles . . . Toronto.' A message was scrawled in a bold hand on the reverse side. 'Am interested in discussing a business project with you. Meet me at the following address tomorrow morning ten a.m.' An address followed, nothing more. Ashley felt her temper rising. Fat arrogant twit! He evidentially expected her to be overwhelmed at the mere thought of meeting him since he had not even left a phone number to call if she wanted to refuse.

'Stage-door Johnny, is it?' Bob's old eyes were inquisitive.

'What?'

'Must be some admirer, the way you're blushing!'

Ashley became even redder. 'No, just some . . . some idiot,' she said. She was about to tear up the card, but thought better of it. She'd have to let her agent know about it, that was only ethical. She tucked the offending card into her shoulder bag and wishing Bob an abrupt goodnight stalked briskly to the Underground station.

Before she got back to her shabby bedsitter in Swiss Cottage she phoned her agent from a public phone booth. She didn't want to disturb the rest of her house by making late-night phone calls from the pay phone in the hall. And knowing Gus's volubility she guessed it would be a lengthy one. She arranged her coins in a neat stack and dialled Gus's home number.

Gus had been her agent since she had left drama school. He had come to see the final play the school put on with the graduating class. Ashley had played the lead, and Gus had suggested he represent her for a year's trial to 'see how we get on, my dove'. She had checked with Equity, and been assured that Gus Abrahams was one of the most honest in the business, and while he wasn't a top-flight agent he was nothing to be ashamed of, so she had signed with him. He was in his fifties, a fat gargoyle of a man with a rich cockney accent and an extravagant collection of endearments. He treated Ashley with avuncular affection mingled with theatrical camaraderie. His advice about her career had been sound, and she trusted his opinion.

His phone rang several times before he answered, and she was about to give up when she heard the pips and she dropped the coins into the machine.

'Hi, Gus! It's Ashley.'

'Hello, my treasure. Anything wrong?'

'No. Sorry to call so late, but . . .'

'You can call any time, darling, you know that. I only just got 'ome, as a matter of fact. Been seeing that new play at the Court. Proper load of old rubbish! I dunno what the theatre's coming to . . .'

Knowing Gus's habit of carrying on at length about the state of British theatre, and aware that her stack of coins was limited, Ashley interrupted.

'Yes . . . but, Gus, I'm in a phone box.'

'Sorry, my angel!'

'I would've called tomorrow, but there won't be time. A man called Lucas Martineaux came to see the play tonight . . .'

'Martineaux?' Gus said breathlessly. 'Lucas Martineaux the film director?'

'Yes. He left a note backstage. He wants to see me tomorrow morning and . . .'

'Ashley, my treasure! That's wonderful . . .' the warning pips interrupted Ashley's irritable interjection. She fed more coins into the box. Gus was still talking.

'. . . very talented man indeed. You come and see me the minute you've had your interview . . . or do you want me to come with you?'

'Gus, you don't seem to understand,' Ashley said firmly, 'I don't want to see this Mr Martineaux at all. I don't like the sound of him.'

There was a moment's silence at the end of the line, then: 'What the devil do you mean, Ashley?' said Gus, the jocularity gone from his voice.

'Well, he sounds so arrogant . . . so demanding and . . .'

'Who the 'ell cares what he sounds like?' Gus's voice was up several decibels. 'He's one of the best filmmakers around today, my petal. He doesn't have to try to win any charm contest. You should be thanking your lucky stars . . .'

'But, Gus! I'm not *interested* in being in films!'

'*Why the 'ell not?*' Gus bellowed. Ashley tried to speak, but he continued, 'Who the devil do you think you are, my dove?' The pips sounded again. 'Damn them bloody pips!' He was apoplectic now. 'What's the number in that box?' he demanded. 'I'll call you there.'

She gave him the number and hung up. She was also shaking with rage. But she had to admit Gus had a point. Also he was her agent, and naturally enough wanted her to make money. How could she explain to him that she felt film acting was just too easy? She knew she had a lot to learn, but not in films. She frankly believed film acting was—just luck and the right kind of face.

When the phone rang and Gus came on the line he seemed calmer. 'Now you listen to me, my angel,' he said. 'You go and see Lucas Martineaux tomorrow morning, and you find out what he wants. Tell him you'll think about it, and then come straight round to the office and we'll discuss it.'

'But, Gus!' she pleaded.

'No "buts", lovey. What jobs do you have lined up after your play closes Saturday?'

'You said there was a possibility of playing Cecily in *The Importance of Being Earnest*' at Windsor,' she reminded him.

'A *possibility* only,' he said, 'besides, do you know what they pay at Windsor compared to the salary you'd get making a picture?'

'I'm not interested in working only for the money, Gus,' Ashley told him loftily, 'you know that.'

'Strange as it may seem, my beauty, neither am I,' he replied with dignity. 'Martineaux's films aren't exactly porno flicks, you know. How many of his have you seen?'

'I haven't seen any, as a matter of fact,' she was forced to confess.

'Then let me tell you that they're first-rate, my

treasure, *first rate*. Any actress worth the name would give her eye teeth for a chance to work with him. Particularly an inexperienced newcomer like you.' He waited to see if this hit home.

'Very well, Gus, I'll go and see him. But I won't promise anything,' she added stubbornly.

'Why don't you wait till you're asked, my lady?' He was still angry with her. 'I'm going to bed now, Ashley. I'll see you in the morning.'

After he had hung up Ashley stood in the musty phone box trying to regain her composure. It hadn't occurred to her that her agent would know so much about this film man, nor have such respect for him. 'Just the same, I won't do anything . . . *anything* . . . that I don't want to,' she muttered furiously to herself, and stamped home in a very bad temper indeed.

It hadn't improved much the following morning. Determined to present a serious appearance befitting a young actress intent on a career devoted to 'art for art's sake', she dressed herself in a plain navy blue suit—a mistake, bought a year ago and hardly worn—and under the suit she buttoned her plain white blouse up to her chin. She looked so severe she could have been mistaken for a novice in a religious order. She wore no make-up or jewellery, and pulled her bright hair back into a heavy bun. Even her high-heeled black pumps and sheer nylons did little to relieve the stern front she presented.

She found the office building without any trouble. She was irrationally let down because it seemed modest for a movie czar. Her prejudice demanded an office the size of Buckingham Palace, resplendent with chrome and plate glass, and vulgar in every way. She comforted herself that this was a rented suite. No doubt back in Toronto—or Los Angeles, or wherever he conducted his affairs, his place of business would be as awful as she imagined. Here the plain frosted glass door was merely engraved with the number and a small sign which read: 'Ring and enter.'

In a burst of irritated energy Ashley rang and thrust the door open simultaneously. There was a deafening clatter of metal as numerous film cans hit the polished wooden floor, spewing their ribbon-like contents in all directions. A young man, who had been carrying the cans and who had been hit in the back by Ashley's energetic entry, uttered an oath and turned a pair of furious jet black eyes on her.

'You clumsy, stupid little fool!' he roared.

'I . . . I'm terribly sorry . . .' She knelt down to help retrieve some of the spilled film.

'*Don't touch that!*' She dropped the reel of film as if it had burnt her. 'That's all I need,' he snapped, still raging, 'your fingerprints all over the film. Keep your hands *off*! You've done enough damage already!'

The young man crouched his considerable height down and started carefully rewinding the spools, holding the centre of each reel in his long fingers with caution. Ashley stood and watched him. Even bent over his task he appeared very tall. On closer inspection she realised he was not as young as she had first supposed. There was a fine net of lines around his dark eyes, and his mouth, set at the moment in exasperation, was not the mouth of a boy. Nor was he handsome in the conventional sense. His jutting nose was too hawklike, and the contours of his tanned face too craggy. Rather he would be described as possessing a strong, intensely masculine face. His hair was jet black and fell in unruly locks over his broad forehead. He was wearing faded jeans, battered running shoes, and she could see a checked red and white shirt under the old denim jacket that emphasised his powerful shoulders.

He carefully stacked the remaining cans, some still spilling their contents, on a table, then turned to her.

'Where did you learn to make entrances like that?' he asked laconically. 'On the playing fields of Rugby?'

'I was miles away,' Ashley muttered, embarrassed.

'You sure came back with a wallop,' he said. 'You dented a couple of the cans.' Ashley remained silent. 'Don't look so worried—I think they'll recover.' His face was implacable, and she couldn't figure out whether he was teasing or not. 'What can I do for you, young lady?'

His voice had a pleasant drawl when he wasn't shouting. American, perhaps? She couldn't place it. She wondered what position he held in the Martineaux set-up. Errand boy? Messenger? Hardly. In spite of his shabby clothes he exuded an air of authority. She didn't visualise him at anybody's beck and call. He was staring at her now, his eyes appraising, no longer angry. She felt the blood rising to her face, a rosy tide.

'I . . . I have an appointment with Mr Martineaux,' she explained, hoping to break the tension that was building between them.

He glanced briefly at his watch—a very expensive one, she noticed. 'Of course! You're not a blonde, then?' he said inexplicably. He continued staring at her in a dispassionate way which she found most disconcerting. She gave a nervous giggle. Again she tried to break the tension.

'Isn't Mr Martineaux here yet?'

'What?'

She pointed to the closed door of the inner office. 'Mr Martineaux. I take it he hasn't arrived yet?'

A grin spread over his face. 'Do you?' he said.

'He must be late.' She fiddled with her gloves. 'I suppose that's the way with film moguls.'

'With *what*?'

'Film moguls.' He stared at her in astonishment. 'Big Hollywood directors,' she explained. 'They think they're too grand to be on time.'

'Do they indeed! Tell me more.' There was a glint in his eyes.

'Well, I've never actually met one,' she confessed, nervousness making her babble, 'but I've a pretty shrewd idea what they're like.'

'Have you?' His well-defined mouth tilted in amusement. 'Well, let's see if your intuition's on target. Describe Lucas Martineaux.'

'Describe him? Oh, I couldn't!'

'Come on,' he said relentlessly, 'you said you knew what he was like.'

'Well, all right . . . he's . . . he's old . . .'

One of his strong black eyebrows arched. 'How old?' he asked.

'Oh, I don't know exactly. Sort of middle-aged . . . greyish . . .'

'Greyish, eh?' He covered his mouth with his hand.

'*Definitely* greyish.' This attractive man was beginning to assume the role of an accomplice. 'And fat.'

'*Fat?*'

'Certainly. All those business lunches,' Ashley was getting into her stride now, 'and probably bald . . . and . . . and smokes cigars,' she finished triumphantly.

He threw back his head and laughed. His teeth were even and startlingly white in his tanned face. 'I'm happy to say you're wrong on all counts, Miss Morrison,' he said, 'although I did gain a couple of pounds last Christmas.'

'How do you know my name?' she asked, startled.

'You have a ten o'clock appointment. Right?' She nodded, a horrible suspicion dawning. 'And like a fool I was expecting a blonde. You were blonde in the play last night.'

Her huge eyes turned green with dismay. 'Oh God! You're not . . . ?'

He nodded cheerfully. 'Lucas Martineaux,' he admitted. 'Allow me to introduce myself. I should have told you right away, but I didn't recognise you.'

Ashley turned pink with indignation. 'You encouraged me!' she protested. 'You had no right . . .'

'None at all,' he smiled charmingly, 'but I was having such a good time I couldn't resist it.'

'I don't enjoy being made a fool of,' she said with icy dignity.

'I don't blame you. But you didn't seem a bit foolish, Miss Morrison. Prejudiced perhaps, prone to cast in stereotypes, but not foolish.' His eyes twinkled with mischief. 'I apologise—I behaved badly. Now what do you say I make us some coffee before you explode?' For Ashley was scarlet with humiliation and fury.

He opened the door to the other room. Apart from a large desk covered in files and papers, a phone and an easy chair, it didn't look any different from the ante-room.

'No coffee for me, thank you,' she said coldly, throw-ing off her winter coat and sweeping past him to sit primly on the edge of the proffered easy chair.

'Still mad, eh?' The wretched man didn't seem in the least put out. He busied himself with an electric kettle and carefully measured instant coffee into a navy blue ceramic mug. He didn't try to persuade her to change her mind and join him. Secretly she longed for a cup of coffee, but she would have died of thirst before accept-ing one from him.

He plugged in the kettle, then perched himself on the edge of the desk and looked down at her.

'Before I explain why I wanted to see you, Miss Morrison, I must tell you how impressed I was by your performance last night,' he said. He was all seriousness now, the teasing of a moment before had vanished. His eyes, so dark a brown they looked almost black, had lost their twinkle. Ashley wondered how she could ever have mistaken him for anything but an executive.

'Thank you.' She was as wintry as the January day outside.'

'I understand you only recently graduated from drama school.'

'Seven months ago.'

'I thought as much,' he said. She was disconcerted. Had her performance been *that* raw? 'You have a certain . . . unspoiled quality,' he bit his lip for a minute. 'It's hard to describe,' he said, 'but you have a kind of . . . freshness. Well, coming for this interview dressed like that, for example,' he gestured to her suit, 'with your hair drawn off your face so that I can see the bones. No make-up hiding your freckles. Those freckles will photo-graph a treat. A cameraman's dream.' She could have killed him.

The kettle was boiling, so he left his perch to pour hot water over the coffee powder in his mug, then he returned to the desk and picked up a thick manuscript from the pile of papers.

'This is the scenario of a movie I'm starting to shoot next month,' he told her. 'It's about an English family in Canada in the 1700s. I'll be shooting in Canada—in Ontario and Quebec—and there's a part in it for you. The role of the only daughter. It's not the lead, but it's a featured role, and it's dramatic. After seeing you in the play last night I know you're right for it. Now that I see you're a redhead, I'm positive.'

Ashley looked at him antagonistically. 'What's the character like?' she asked.

'Kind of . . . feisty. She's not sugar and spice.' He took a sip of coffee and peered at her over the rim of the mug. His eyes were fringed with extremely long lashes and Ashley found herself gazing at them. She blushed hotly and hastily looked away.

'Well, Miss Morrison, what do you say?' He put down the mug and leaned across the desk. 'Are you interested?'

'No!' It came out far more abruptly than she intended.

'It can't be because I pulled that dumb stunt when you arrived? That's not the reason, is it?'

'No, Mr Martineaux, that's not the reason.'

'You're not free for February and possibly March?'

Ashley was tempted to say she was doing *The Importance of Being Earnest* then, but she knew that wasn't strictly true. Besides, she wanted to take Lucas Martineaux down a peg, let him know that she wasn't bowled over by his offer.

'As far as I know I'm quite free.'

'But?' he asked tersely.

'I'm just starting in this business and I want to go on learning,' she replied levelly.

'Naturally.'

'Well, I don't think I'd learn anything making a picture.'

Lucas Martineaux had very expressive eyebrows. At this juncture they expressed disdain. 'May one ask you why not?' he said.

'Because it would be too easy,' she blurted. 'I need to be challenged.'

His eyes became hooded. 'You don't think playing an important part in a feature movie would be a challenge to you?' His voice was deceptively smooth.

'Frankly, no.' She raised her chin defiantly. 'I'm a theatre person. I'm serious about my profession.'

Lucas Martineaux flung the script on to the desk with a crash. 'You're also the most ignorant, conceited little bore I've ever met.' Ashley quailed before his rage. 'Not learn anything! Do you know what an opportunity you're turning down? Not because it's *my* picture, but because you're wet behind the ears. You know nothing. Believe me,' he hissed, 'your attitude shows that you're nothing but a rank amateur. Well, I could accept that, everyone has to start somewhere. But you haven't even the grace to admit you could learn something from films. You have the gall . . . the unmitigated *gall* . . . to think you're too good for the movies! Don't say another thing,' he raged when Ashley helplessly tried to interject. 'I'd appreciate it if you stopped wasting my time and went about your business!'

He strode to the outer door and flung it open, then stood, his broad shoulders silhouetted against the glass. Inwardly quaking but determined to present a bold front, Ashley folded her coat over her arm and walked out into the corridor. As she passed him he said cuttingly:

'That quality I said the part needed . . . it's bloody-mindedness . . . it would have suited you to a T.' On that he slammed the door.

Ashley pressed the lift button with trembling fingers. She was a fair-minded girl and she had the nasty sensation that he had right on his side. She was forced to admit that her reasons for refusing the part did sound priggish. But it was impossible to explain to someone who worked in films how she felt. Besides, she reasoned, to still her conscience, it would do an arrogant man like him good to meet an actress who didn't fall all over him just because he could offer her a well-paid job.

She reluctantly made her way to her appointment with Gus. She didn't relish reporting the interview, and she heartily wished Lucas Martineaux had never set foot in the theatre last night. He disturbed her, and it wasn't just because of the unpleasant scene she had experienced. He possessed a quality she had never encountered before, an animal magnetism that both intrigued and alarmed her. When she searched in her purse for change for her ticket she came across his card with his curt request for their meeting. She tore it into a myriad pieces and dropped them into a litter-bin. She only wished the echo of his wrath could be disposed of as easily.

She didn't go into the details of her disastrous interview to Gus. She merely told him they hadn't hit it off, and she doubted the film director would want to work with her. Gus didn't say much—apart from pointing out that she couldn't always expect to like her director—but she could tell from the absence of his usual florid endearments that he was disappointed in her, and this made her angrier with Lucas Martineaux than ever.

The play closed the following Saturday. Ashley was still feeling upset, so to cheer herself up she bought a new dress for the closing night party. Striped grey and white gauzey cotton, it had a full skirt and huge bell-like sleeves that were gathered into tight cuffs at the wrist. The bodice was yoked with a demure starched broderie anglaise bib ruffled round the seams. The demureness was deceptive, for the white bib opened in a deep vee which showed the gentle swell of her breasts against the crisp cotton. She wore a wide black patent belt round her narrow waist, and high-heeled strap sandals. When she danced she was pleasantly aware that the hem of her frilled petticoat flashed like white foam. Her hair, which she wore loose and curling, seemed the colour of polished mahogany against the pale grey and white cotton. But even the frank admiration of the male members of the company, plus the knowledge that she looked particularly attractive, didn't lift the irritable cloud she seemed to have been living under since her meeting with the dark, arrogant film director.

This was her first experience of the end of a run too,

and she found it sad. Like the breaking up of a family. For when the company has been a happy one—as was the case in *Elizabeth the Queen*—the closing party always contains a hint of sadness mingled with the festivities.

When the dawn came and the party finally came to an end there was a flurry of exchanged addresses. Actors vowed to 'keep in touch, darling', but Ashley sensed, correctly, that this comradeship was born out of nostalgia for the enterprise just finished and the emotional feeling generated by a room full of actors. In a week all the promises to write or phone would be forgotten, and a new play or film or television show would be the focal point of their lives. *Elizabeth the Queen* would be just another credit on the résumé.

This was a facet of show business Ashley found increasingly distasteful. The extravagant vows of undying friendship, the emotional hyperbole was a sham she shrank from. She knew full well that such protestations had the substance of moonbeams.

She phoned Gus the following morning, to be told there were no auditions planned for the immediate future. She was well and truly out of work—or 'resting', to use an old theatrical euphemism. She decided on the spur of the moment that she needed to escape from the city and renew herself in the country. So that very afternoon she boarded the train that would take her home for a short visit to her beloved Cotswold Hills. Perhaps home, unlike the new dress or the party, would have the power to dispel the gloom that stubbornly clung to her like mist.

CHAPTER TWO

THE moment Aunt Constance met her at the station Ashley knew something was wrong—not that her aunt said anything, that wasn't her style, but, like Ashley's, her homely face also reflected all her emotions, and right now it was furrowed with anxiety.

While they were driving to the cottage in the battered family Mini Ashley cautiously asked: 'Is Mother all right, Auntie Con?'

Ashley's mother suffered from a severe heart condition, and the least worry or exertion was dangerous for her. Since her husband's death ten years before her health had steadily declined. It was then that Constance Morrison had given up her small dressmaking business and come to live with her ailing sister-in-law and ten-year-old niece.

'She's fine, Ashley. She's waiting to have tea with you before her rest. Now don't chat, child! You know I need to concentrate when I'm driving.' And Ashley, familiar with her aunt's ways, bided her time in silence.

When they arrived she was ecstatically greeted by Muppet, her little rough-haired dog, a charming animal of dubious ancestry, who seemed in danger of wagging his tail off, so extreme was his delight. With affection she watched her mother's wan face, lit with pride now as she listened to her daughter's backstage stories and description of the closing night party.

After tea, a splendid one of anchovy toast and home-made walnut cake to celebrate Ashley's return, she again asked her aunt if anything was wrong. Mrs Morrison had retired to her room to rest and Ashley and her aunt were washing the tea things in the small scullery which looked out over fields that led to a small spinney. This time Aunt Constance did not refuse to answer. Thoughtfully she rinsed the blue flowered milk-jug and handed it to her niece.

'We're in a bit of trouble, Ashley,' she said. 'I was hoping I wouldn't have to burden you with it, but . . .'

Ashley's grey eyes filled with alarm. 'It's not Mother?' All her life she had lived with the reality of yet another setback in her uncomplaining mother's health. But she was still unable to control the lurch of fear that clutched her every time she was faced with this knowledge.

'Well, she's not getting any better, Ashley. She never will—we both know that.' Constance's tone was brisk, but she knew her aunt well enough to recognise that this was merely a mask for deep affection and concern. Ashley finished drying the jug and waited patiently for her aunt to continue.

'Remember those shares your father bought, just before he died?' Aunt Constance went on. Ashley nodded. 'Well, they're not exactly thriving, and what with the cost of living . . .' She emptied the soapy water and dried her work-worn hands. 'To put it bluntly, child, we're . . . broke, I think you call it. Heaven knows we never had any money to spare in the past, but now we can't even meet our expenses.'

'But Daddy bought those shares so we'd be looked after in the future,' Ashley protested.

Constance put her arm round her niece's shoulder.

'My brother was a fine man and a splendid vicar,' she said, 'but he was terrible at business, Ashley. Those shares are worthless.'

Ashley blinked hard several times. 'What are we going to do, Auntie Con?'

'Well, I'm taking in as much sewing as I can,' Constance replied matter-of-factly, 'but this is a small village and the demand for my services isn't exactly overwhelming. We can't live on my earnings, I'm afraid.'

'I'll get a job,' Ashley volunteered. 'I can get work in Castleford and live here at home.'

'And just what will you *do*, my dear?' Aunt Constance started putting away the pretty blue and white china, an old-fashioned pattern of cornflowers and ivy leaves that had been part of the household for as long as Ashley could remember. 'Castleford doesn't have a theatre, as I recall.'

'Not a job in the theatre. A proper job . . . in a shop, or an office,' Ashley finished lamely.

'And what about your stage work?' Her aunt fixed her with a pair of faded blue eyes, sharp as gimlets. 'Do you intend to throw away all that training and talent?'

'It's not that important, Auntie Con,' Ashley lied, her gaze wavering under that relentless blue stare. 'It's been fun, but I wouldn't miss it a bit.'

'Fiddlesticks, Ashley! Don't try and hoodwink me, my girl. Save your theatricals for the stage.'

'Well, I have to do *something*,' Ashley flared. 'I just can't ignore the situation.'

Constance sighed heavily. 'Losing our temper isn't going to help us, child,' she said, 'and neither is your working in a shop. You'd never earn enough to keep the three of us. And somebody has to stay here to look after your mother, so I can't take a job.'

'What if you and Mother moved to a larger town? Could you make enough doing dressmaking at home then? With what I can contribute, of course.'

'I've thought of that,' her aunt responded, 'in fact I discussed it with Dr Shaunessy. But he says it would be fatal to move your mother to another environment. The upheaval would be too much for her.' Constance's usually straight shoulders drooped, and she looked older than Ashley had ever remembered. I must do something, Ashley thought helplessly. Gus must get me a well-paid job *fast*. Not a modest repertory job, but something that pays a lot of money. Something like . . .

'Of course!' she exclaimed aloud. 'Of course, that's the answer!' She grabbed her aunt's bony shoulders and hugged her tight. 'I'm such a fool—I completely forgot about Mr Martineaux's film!'

'What are you talking about, child?' Aunt Constance shook herself free from Ashley's embrace. 'What's all this about a film?'

'There's a chance I'm going to be in a film,' Ashley told her, 'and it'll pay *lots*, so you won't have to worry

. . . at least not for a while.' She did some rapid mental calculations. She wasn't exactly sure of the amount involved, but she knew it was considerable compared to legitimate theatre salaries. If she was extra careful about expenditures she should be able to save enough for them to coast for six months or so, which would give them breathing space while they sorted out their next move.

'Why in heaven's name didn't you mention it before?' Her aunt eyed her suspiciously.

Why indeed? Ashley thought, coming down to earth with a bump, because I've probably ruined my chances with Lucas Martineaux for good and all. But all she said to Aunt Con was, 'It's bad luck in the theatre to talk about things until the contract's signed.'

'Well, when will you know? At least tell me that.' A gleam of hope shone in the older woman's eyes.

'I . . . er . . . I'm not sure. In fact I'd better phone Gus now and check with him . . . er . . . to see if he's heard anything,' said Ashley, feeling less and less confident. It had seemed the obvious solution at the moment, but recalling Lucas Martineaux's angry command to 'go about your business', it seemed unlikely he would reconsider and offer her the part again. But she couldn't resist that faint gleam of hope in Aunt Con's worried blue eyes, so she closeted herself in the living room to phone Gus.

In fairness to him she had to explain the situation and her sudden need for money. But she made him promise not to tell Lucas Martineaux her reasons, just to move heaven and earth to get her the part. Gus promised to do his best, but he didn't sound very hopeful, and Ashley hung up with a sinking heart.

'No news yet,' she said with forced gaiety to Auntie Con. 'Gus is going to call me tomorrow so we'll just have to be patient, darling. How about a game of Scrabble?' But she found it impossible to practice what she preached, and her attention constantly wandered from the Scrabble game, so that after an hour she excused herself and pretended to read a book until bedtime.

The following morning she was so edgy waiting for

Gus's call that she forced herself to take Muppet for a long tramp in the spinney in spite of an icy downpour that turned the fields to chocolate brown mud, and whipped her face until her cheeks glowed pink with cold. Muppet, his usually tousled coat sleeked seal-smooth with rain, barked joyously while he and his young mistress ran slipping and sliding in the boggy fields, scrambling over the ditch and into the creaking spinney, to play hide-and-seek round the dripping trees until both girl and dog were drenched and breathless.

Happily exhausted at last, they returned to the cottage, and she was taking off her muddy Wellington boots in the scullery when the phone rang.

'It's for you, Ashley,' her aunt called. Tugging off her left boot, Ashley dashed to answer it. It was Gus.

'He wants to see you,' he said.

'Wh—what? Who does?' She stood, dripping on to the faded carpet, her fire-bright hair plastered to her head, unable to function normally, to take in what her agent was saying.

'Martineaux. He wants to see you, my treasure. Says he won't discuss it with me until he's seen you again. Says he wants to "reaffirm your type", whatever *that* means.'

Ashley's heart sank. Lucas Martineaux had made it pretty clear just what he thought her type was, and it wasn't complimentary.

'You're to be at the Savoy Hotel tomorrow morning at ten,' Gus was saying. 'The part's still not cast, so there's a chance yet.'

'The Savoy Hotel?'

'That's where he's staying. He'll meet you in the Savoy Grill. All right?'

'All right.' She couldn't resist asking, 'Do you think there's a chance, Gus?'

'Don't ask me, my poppet,' Gus replied unhelpfully. 'He sounded very cool on the blower, I must say. But he wants to see you, and that's a step in the right direction. All I can say is "good luck", my petal. Let me know how it goes.'

'I will . . . and . . . thanks, Gus.' When Ashley hung up she discovered she was shaking. And it wasn't from the cold. It was from apprehension at the thought of meeting Lucas Martineaux again. She still remembered the fury of those piercing black eyes, and it still gave her the shivers.

Before she took the afternoon train back to London to prepare for tomorrow's interview, Mrs Morrison, horrified by her daughter's soaking wet hair and clothes, insisted on a hot bath and some soup to ward off a chill. Aunt Constance vociferously supported her.

'Out of those wet things and into a hot bath right away, child—and no arguments. Much chance you'll have of getting a job if you get pneumonia!' She had lovingly bullied her niece this way since she'd taken over their household, but now Ashley sensed the eagerness behind her words. This was not just *any* part Ashley was trying for; it was their immediate salvation. Ashley hoped against hope that the saturnine film director wasn't one to harbour grudges, and that his request for this interview wasn't just a chance for him to humiliate her.

On the dot of ten the following morning Ashley entered the elegant portals of the Savoy Grill. Outwardly she looked as composed as if she had just signed a five-year-film contract and hadn't a worry in the world. Inwardly she was a quaking jelly. For this meeting she had dressed with care and was looking particularly fashionable in a pair of green tweed knickerbockers and matching jacket with braided frogs and dull silver buttons. One of Aunt Constance's talents was to turn the most unlikely garments into clothes that looked as if they had stepped out of the pages of *Vogue*. This chic outfit was made out of an old suit of the Reverend Morrison's. It was a great favourite of Ashley's, her 'lucky suit', she called it. She just prayed it wouldn't let her down this morning.

She smoothed the fine green wool stockings on her slim calves, brushed a minuscule speck of dust from her buckled pumps, and fluffing the cream lace jabot at her throat, seated herself to wait for Lucas Martineaux.

She didn't recognise him when he first arrived. Gone
was the rumpled jean-clad figure she expected, and
instead an immaculate business man stood before her.
His exquisitely cut dark suit was impeccable. His shirt
was snow white and silk, like his tie, which gave a touch
of discreet colour to his otherwise rather sombre ensem-
ble. His hair had been tamed from its unruly shock to a
lustrous cap of jet black curls that gleamed blue where
the light caught them. But his eyes were unchanged.
They were as cold and hard as steel.

'Oh! . . . Oh, it's you!' she blurted, completely taken
aback by his unexpected elegance.

'Good morning, Miss Morrison,' he said icily, seating
himself on the plum-coloured velvet chair beside her. A
waiter hovered, but Lucas did not beckon him.
Apparently there was no question of coffee at this
meeting. 'You're prompt,' he continued, 'I'll say that for
you.' He managed to make it sound insulting.

'I realise your time is valuable,' countered Ashley.
She tried to sound pleasant—she needed the job—but
nevertheless there was an edge to her voice. His hostility
was catching, and it was hard for her to disguise the fact
that she disliked him just as much as he did her.

'As you are aware, your agent phoned me yesterday,'
he said, 'and I asked you to meet me here because I want
an explanation.' Completely at a loss, she stared into his
ice-black eyes. 'I think I'm owed an explanation,' he
repeated. 'You were very definite in your refusal of my
original offer. Now Mr Abrahams tells me you're interested in playing the role after all. I'd like to know
what changed your mind.'

Never a good liar, Ashley found herself groping for
words. 'Well, I . . . I . . . er . . . I thought over what you
told me, and . . . er . . . thought perhaps I'd been too
. . . too hasty.'

'Come off it, Miss Morrison!' he said scathingly.
'Don't give me that! You can do better. You're not the
sort of girl who changes her mind every five minutes.
What's the *real* reason?'

She lowered her eyes before his invincible stare. Her lashes, lightly mascaraed for this meeting, fanned against her cheek. 'I need the money,' she answered quietly.

'That's more like it. Greed!' His triumph burnt like acid. 'What do you need the money *for*?'

'None of your business!' she flared. For a moment she wondered if she should tell him the truth, fling herself on his mercy, but pride restrained her. It was bad enough having to eat humble pie and beg for work in his wretched film, without turning herself into an object of pity. 'I've . . . over-extended myself,' she said grandly, lifting her eyes, which were green as glass by now.

He chuckled, and the sound was not attractive to Ashley.

'And you're willing to slum, are you? To work in a lowly film to pay your debts?' He was relentless.

Ashley couldn't think of anything to say, apart from apologising for the other day, and she wasn't about to do that. So she contented herself by giving him an imperious glare.

'Well, you run true to type, Ashley, after all,' he said enigmatically. This was the first time he had used her Christian name, but there was no warmth in his voice. If anything he sounded more scornful than before.

'True to type? I don't understand?'

'Extravagance and actresses—the two go together.' His lips twisted into a bitter smile. 'What did you squander your money on? Jewellery? Parties? Judging from that trendy outfit you've got on, my guess is that you've bought too many expensive clothes. Don't look so mortified,' he added with disgust. 'You wouldn't be the first actress to go into debt for the sake of appearance. Actresses aren't noted for their good sense, you know.'

She stifled an indignant protest and kept silent. Better to say nothing. She wouldn't get trapped that way, even if it did seem like an admission of guilt.

'How old are you, Ashley?' he asked, his voice suddenly weary.

'Nearly twenty-one,' she said.

'How nearly?'

'In six months,' she admitted reluctantly.

'A kid, in fact. A stupid spoilt kid who's got herself into a jam and can't handle it.'

Again she prevented herself protesting this injustice. The effort of keeping silent made her blush scarlet. Mistaking this as an admission of guilt, he went on:

'Well, you're in luck, young lady. It so happens that I have a soft heart . . . also I've not been able to find anyone to fill the role.'

Ashley suspected this second statement was closer to the truth, but with the information that the role was still not cast hope flickered within her and she discreetly bit back the caustic retort she was tempted to make.

'So I will again offer you the part.'

Relief overwhelmed her. She gripped the edge of her chair and blinked her enormous grey eyes rapidly several times. 'Thank you,' she said tremulously.

'Before you get all misty-eyed,' he continued nastily, 'let me point out that I'm not doing this as a favour to you. I'd use some other actress if I could, don't kid yourself. But I've no more time to go on searching. And you do have the right quality.'

'Mmm! Bloody-mindedness,' she deadpanned.

Lucas Martineaux raised an eyebrow, then allowed himself to grin briefly, but it was a momentary ray of sunshine. His craggy face quickly assumed its former disdainful expression and he went on: 'I have to catch the plane back to Toronto this afternoon, so you've got me over a barrel. Just thank your lucky stars.'

'I do,' she assured him.

He ignored this. 'I want you to understand that this film isn't going to be easy to shoot. We'll be doing a lot of exterior work in bad weather and rough conditions. You won't be pampered on a film set the way you are in the theatre.'

'I understand.'

'Stop interrupting!' he barked. 'You do *not* have the remotest idea of what this shoot is going to be like.

You're totally ignorant of this medium, and I don't want any temperaments and tantrums from you when the going gets tough. Understood?'

Fury drained the blood from her face. She drew herself upright in her chair and said, her voice trembling in spite of herself, 'I have *never* had a tantrum onstage in my life, Mr Martineaux. I may be a beginner, but that's not my fault. My attitude to my work is totally professional. You're being grossly unfair to assume that I'll behave badly simply because you don't like me.'

He stared at her, his lips set in a terse line, but with a hint of respect in his sloe-dark eyes. 'OK!' he said finally, 'just so we understand each other. I don't want you complaining later on that you didn't realise what you were getting into.'

'I realise very well,' she said. 'I'm not expecting it to be a picnic.' Particularly with you in charge, she added silently.

'Just so long as you don't have any illusions,' he said. 'It's a very lucky break for you, young lady. You'll be working with very good people—experienced pro's, all of them. The star of the movie is Sloane Sheppard.' He looked at Ashley antagonistically. 'I suppose you've heard of her? Even in your superior world of the theatre?'

Ashley bit her full lower lip in vexation. 'I've heard of Sloane Sheppard,' she said tightly, 'and for what it's worth I admire her very much.'

'Then you have good judgment,' he said. 'You'll be able to learn a lot from Sloane. Don't waste the opportunity. Now—to business. My producer will contact Mr Abrahams about the contract and the plane tickets, and my P.A. will see to it that you get a copy of the scenario.' He stood up, terminating further discussion. Ashley would like to have known what a P.A. was, but had no intention of asking him and leaving herself open to more remarks about her abysmal ignorance.

He held out his hand and she noticed that he wore a gold signet ring with a dark green stone set in it on his

little finger, and that his nails were remarkably clean and
well-shaped. When Ashley put her hand in his she felt a
small shock, like a tiny electric jolt. His grip was firm,
the flesh of his palm warm and dry. Irrationally her hand
felt safe in his.

'Welcome aboard, Ashley,' he said. 'I can't honestly
say I'm looking forward to working with you, but if you
toe the line we should get along without too many
hassles.'

She pulled her small hand hastily from his. 'Goodbye,
Mr Martineaux,' she said through gritted teeth, 'see you
in Canada.'

She swept out of the room quivering with rage. If
she'd stayed in his presence another moment she would
have hit him! Then the job would have been lost for sure!
That precious, well-paid job. She would have given
anything to throw it right back in his teeth, but that was a
luxury she couldn't afford. She would just have to
somehow live through the next few weeks trying to ignore Lucas Martineaux and his detestable personality
—although she suspected ignoring Lucas Martineaux
was easier said than done. His personality might be
repellant, but it was very powerful. She had never met
anyone who maddened her so much. She strode through
the January chill to Gus's office trying to feel elated by
her success, but feeling only intense irritation at the
prospect of working for this infuriating man.

Everyone else seemed to be delighted that she was
making this film. Gus was happy with the contract,
which was even more generous than they'd hoped, and
he showered her with endearments every time he spoke
to her. And her mother and aunt were beside themselves
with pleasure. Mrs Morrison's delicate face became
positively animated everytime she mentioned *Time of
Trial*, the title of Lucas's film in which Ashley was to play
the part of Elizabeth.

The script was a source of confusion to Ashley,
although she admired its dramatic tension. It felt peculiar to be handling an enormous linen-bound manuscript
rather than the neat, small French's editions of plays.

And the content of this unwieldy scenario seemed to consist almost entirely of camera shots with bewildering references like 'shoot Elizabeth's P.O.V.', or 'long dissolve', or 'stock shot', all of which was Double Dutch to her. There seemed to be next to no dialogue on the pages. Each scene was numbered and contained only half a dozen lines. However, there was a lot of visual action, and while studying her role she began to develop an affinity for the headstrong girl she would be portraying.

'It's so exciting, darling,' Mrs Morrison said one afternoon shortly before Ashley was due to fly to Toronto. 'To think this time next week you'll be in Canada working with Sloane Sheppard! You must tell me all about her the moment you have time to write.' Since Ashley's mother was unable to go out she watched a lot of television and had seen the immensely popular Sloane Sheppard many times. She was thrilled that soon she would have a first-hand account of her idol.

'I'll write as soon as I can,' Ashley promised, 'but I've a feeling my nose is going to be kept pretty much to the grindstone. Mr Martineaux seems . . . quite a slave-driver.' She had kept her personal opinion of Lucas to herself, not wanting to utter his hateful name if she could avoid it. But Aunt Constance wasn't so easily put off.

'You've not mentioned the director at all, Ashley,' she said, her needle flying like a silver dart in the firelight. She was busy hemming a dress for Ashley to take to Toronto, for in spite of Ashley's protests she was convinced her niece would require a wardrobe of fashionable clothes while she was in Canada, and had been sewing steadily ever since Ashley had signed the contract. 'I've read about him in the papers. Is he as forceful as they say?'

'He's certainly that,' Ashley answered shortly.

Her aunt looked at her over her glasses. 'Go on, child,' she said, 'describe him.'

'Yes, do, darling,' Ashley's gentle mother chimed in. 'I love hearing about famous people, particularly when you're going to be working with them.'

'Well, he's tall, dark and ugly,' her daughter said with asperity.

Aunt Constance bit off a piece of thread. 'He didn't look ugly in the picture they published in the *Herald*,' she said, 'quite the contrary, in fact. A good strong face.'

'If you like that type,' Ashley muttered.

'I certainly prefer his looks to most of the pretty-pretty faces one sees nowadays,' Aunt Constance replied equably. 'Mr Martineaux looks to me as if he's got plenty of character.'

Ashley was astonished to discover that she was shaking. Just *talking* about the wretched man seemed to drive her into a rage. What was it about him? Even a discussion about his looks upset her. It seemed that his personality was strong enough to exert power over her when he was hundreds of miles away. This was a new experience for Ashley, and she didn't like it.

'He may have character, but it's pretty poisonous,' she said.

'I take it you don't like him, Ashley?' Aunt Constance seemed to find this amusing.

'Oh, darling,' Mrs Morrison looked anxious, 'isn't it going to be very difficult for you, to have to work with someone you dislike?'

'Don't worry about me, Mother,' Ashley replied, giving her mother a hug, 'I'll be all right. Personal feelings don't enter into a working relationship. Lucas Martineaux may have the charm of a rattlesnake, but I won't allow it to interfere with my work.'

'It might even be an advantage,' Aunt Constance murmured.

'How could it be an advantage, Connie?' asked Mrs Morrison.

'I think Ashley needs a firm hand,' Aunt Constance said placidly, ignoring Ashley's outrage. 'This Lucas Martineaux may be able to get a better performance out of her than a weaker man could.'

'Perhaps you'd like him to beat me?' snapped Ashley furiously, two bright pink spots staining her cheeks.

'Spare the rod and spoil the actress—is that your philosophy, Auntie Con?'

'Don't be foolish, child.' Her aunt folded her sewing neatly. 'You always jump to such extremes. And getting into a temper is silly. I merely expressed an opinion, so stop *glowering*!' She turned to her sister-in-law. 'Time for your rest, Hilda dear. Ashley and I will get the supper. Come, Ashley!' she commanded, 'come and work your temper off on the potatoes.'

In the chill scullery she turned to Ashley. 'You must realise that I'm very fond of you, child,' she smiled, 'and anything I say which might be interpreted as a criticism is only said out of love.'

Ashley's temper—of short duration at the best of times—evaporated like mist in the sun. 'I'm sorry I got so cross, Auntie Con,' she gave her aunt a boisterous bear-hug. 'I'm edgy about this film, I suppose.'

'That's only natural,' her aunt agreed. 'Watch that paring knife, dear! It's a new world for you, and an important one. But I must tell you, Ashley, that at times I have doubts about your chosen profession. Doubts as to whether it can bring you lasting happiness, dear child.'

'Don't you think I should be an actress, then?' Ashley asked. She was surprised at Aunt Con's attitude. She had always encouraged Ashley in the past, and had seemed genuinely happy when her niece had won a scholarship to the drama school. True, she didn't always approve of the behaviour of some theatre people, but neither did Ashley. Surely she realised that?

'I don't think you could be anything else,' her aunt went on. 'You have talent, Ashley, a lot of talent. I'm not sure how far you'll go. Only time will tell. But you've chosen a difficult profession, to say the least, my dear. But it's not that part that worries me.' She paused to look out of the small window, as if seeking inspiration from the dripping mists of the January evening. 'I'm sometimes afraid you'll get hurt, dear—hurt beyond healing. You need stability in your life Ashley. You need someone to protect and guide you, someone stable to rely on. There don't seem to be too many of that sort in the theatre.'

Ashley dropped a peeled potato into the saucepan. 'You're afraid I'll fall in love with an actor and he'll ruin my life, is that it, Auntie?' she chuckled.

'Something like that,' her aunt agreed.

'Don't worry, darling,' Ashley tossed her flame-bright head and grinned, 'actors don't attract me one bit. Besides, I've no plans for falling in love. Not for years and years.'

This piece of information didn't seem to appease her aunt, however. 'I certainly hope to see you happily married before I quit this earth, Ashley.' She sounded quite put out. 'That's what I'm trying to say. I want you to have *everything*. And I don't believe the theatre will be enough for you. You need a . . . an emotional centre to your life. You need the security of a home of your own, children, and a good loving husband. A man strong enough to stand up to you when need be, but who will love you through thick and thin. There's passion in you, child, and it would be a tragedy if it was wasted on the wrong man, or frittered away.'

Ashley dried her slender hands and turned to the older woman. 'Maybe one day I'll find all those things, Auntie. But right now I'm just going to concentrate on doing this film . . . all right? And don't worry about me, darling.' Impulsively she kissed her aunt's lined cheek. 'I'm really going to be all right, you know.'

Constance Morrison looked at the vivid heart-shaped face before her. The girl's eyes were so wide and trusting, her mouth the tender mouth of a child. 'I'm probably just an old fool,' Constance said gruffly, 'but I worry. You have burden enough to carry with your mother and me. I'd like to see *you* looked after for a change.'

'I really am capable of looking after myself, Auntie Con,' Ashley assured her.

'No doubt,' her aunt said grimly. 'I'd just like to see you getting some help, that's all.' Abruptly she changed the subject. 'Now, if you've finished those potatoes you can open a bottle of those plums I put up and I'll make a custard.'

Later that night, lying in the narrow bed she had slept in since she was a child, Ashley went over that disquieting conversation again. Deep down she also knew that her career, precious though it was, would not fulfil her all her life. The normalcy of a home and children was a dream she kept hidden in the deepest recesses of her heart. A home, and a husband. She had never really fleshed out this shadowy figure, but she knew full well that he could never be some shallow actor, interested only in the world of the theatre. She had gone out with several young actors, but soon tired of their company. Their absorption with themselves had bored her to tears. And the inevitable skirmish when they had tried to break down her resistance and get her into bed was so predictable. They usually accused her of deep psychological hang-ups—which they eagerly offered to cure by immediately seducing her. It simply didn't seem to sink in that she had a different view of morality which she had no intention of changing for the sake of some casual acquaintance. On occasion she had been called a 'cold-blooded bitch' and worse, so she had finally poured all her energy into her work and kept her dating to the minimum. But she was honest enough to realise that she couldn't spend her life this way. She was a healthy girl, with normal desires and drives that must one day be satisfied. She wouldn't always be able to turn to her work for solace. Both her mind and her body needed the companionship of a male.

But though young, she was wise enough to recognise that casual relationships would never satisfy her, and the chance of meeting the kind of man she wanted among the acting fraternity was slim.

Well, I won't worry about it now, she thought drowsily, pushing her feet against the comfortable solidness of Muppet who had illicitly climbed onto the bed, first I'll get this film over with and put as much money into the kitty as I can, then I'll worry about my romantic future.

Thought of the film immediately conjured up a picture of Lucas Martineaux. This image was so vivid that she opened her grey eyes in alarm, convinced for a sleepy moment that he was standing in the shadowy bedroom glaring down at her. She turned over irritably in the warm bed. 'Go away!' she whispered softly as she slipped into sleep.

But the memory of Lucas was not so easily dismissed, and all through the night her dreams were haunted by the deep harsh planes of his face, and his scornful ink-black eyes.

CHAPTER THREE

ASHLEY watched the fat little ferry-boat chugging away across the cold black waters of the inner harbour of Toronto. The deep pile carpet in the hotel bedroom caressed her bare feet, and a fitful lemony sun cast rays of light on to the beige silk walls of the room she had been ushered into last evening, when she was reeling with jet-lag and excitement.

She had been met at the airport by a smiling woman in her early thirties, who had introduced herself as Maggy McCullam, Lucas's P.A. Ashley had immediately taken to Maggy, and by the time they had arrived at the hotel they were old friends.

'Luc decided to put everybody up at the Harbour Castle,' Maggy explained. 'It's more convenient since he lives on the premises, so to speak.'

'You mean Mr Martineaux lives in a hotel?' She had thought it an odd way to live, but nothing about him would surprise her.

'Not in the hotel,' Maggy had laughed. 'He has one of the condominiums attached to the hotel.'

'Condo . . . ?'

'Apartments . . . *flats*, I guess you call them . . . that you buy. Luc's been living in the Harbour Castle Apartments for years. It's handy to Film House, where his office is, and it's downtown. For a Toronto base it couldn't be better.' By now she had ushered Ashley into the lobby of the hotel.

It had seemed to Ashley's tired eyes about the same size as a modest football field. There were acres of gleaming beige marble, a low fountain played in one corner, and the teak walls were hung with Oriental screens, some carved out of reddish wood inlaid with ivory, some lacquered vivid Chinese red. As its name implied, the hotel was built on the harbour front. The far

39

wall was made entirely of glass and overlooked the lake, which was now a dark metal colour in the late evening light. She could just make out a black hump of land, like a whale's back, on the other side of the channel and assumed this was the far shore.

When she had sketchily unpacked Maggy had suggested they have dinner together. To Ashley's relief they ate in the Peppermill Buffet, which was cheaper than any of the other hotel restaurants. This suited her very well since she wanted to send every penny she could back to Aunt Constance in England, and she had planned to eat as cheaply as possible during her stay.

They ordered hamburgers and coffee, and while they were waiting for the food to arrive Maggy had handed her an envelope.

'Here you are, Ashley—your per diems for the first week. Just sign here,' she produced an official-looking sheet, 'then we can both relax.'

Ashley peeped inside the envelope. It seemed to contain a lot of twenty-dollar bills. 'What's this for?' she had asked.

'Why, for your daily expenses . . . food and stuff. Your hotel's paid for by the company.'

Ashley's heart rose. The first opportunity she would open a bank account, put most of the money in it, and send a sizeable cheque off to England. Beaming, she thanked Maggy profusely.

'Don't thank me, honey,' Maggy had said, 'it's the union rules. Just like that work permit we had to get for you, so you could work over here. And speaking of work, here's your schedule. Tomorrow you have a costume fitting in the morning. Make-up consultation at three, and you're to see the hairdresser at the same time. We'll try and arrange for someone to drive you. I'll call you about it in the morning. OK?'

Their hamburgers had arrived—thick patties on white rolls the size of small dinner plates, garnished with tomato slices, onions, various kinds of relish, and a dill pickle. Ashley figured that if the portions were all as generous as this in Canada, she could survive comfortably on one hamburger a day, and save the rest of her money. She had been too excited to do more than peck at the dinner served on the plane, so she had attacked her juicy hamburger with gusto.

Conversation languished while the two girls ate, but over coffee Maggy had lit a cigarette and leaned back in the padded banquette with a sigh of satisfaction.

'Ah, that feels better! I hadn't eaten since breakfast, and that was at seven, so's I could eat with Bobby.'

'Bobby?' queried Ashley.

'My little boy. I won't be seeing much of him when we're shooting, so I try to make up for it now.' Maggy had smiled sheepishly. 'I just happen to have his picture on me. Would you like to see it?'

'I'd love to.' Ashley had taken the proffered picture, which showed a curly-haired boy, holding a large stuffed panda. He was grinning mischievously into the camera. 'He's a darling, Maggy. How old is he?'

'He's seven now, six when that was taken. Luc took it last year.'

'Luc? You mean Lucas Martineaux?' The idea of Lucas taking snapshots of children was somehow out of character. Unless—was it possible that he and Maggy were married?—Married women often kept their own names.

'Your husband . . .' Ashley had said, handing back the photo, 'is he in the film business too?'

Maggy's round face had clouded. 'He was. He was a stunt man. He was killed when Bobby was two.'

Ashley had been filled with compassion. 'I'm sorry, Maggy. It must have been terrible for you.'

'Yeah! It was . . . still is . . . pretty rough. If it hadn't been for Bobby I don't know what I'd have done. And he's so like his dad . . . Bobby's my life, I guess. And I have my work. I enjoy that.'

This had seemed like a good opportunity to ask a question that had been bugging Ashley. 'Talking of your work,' she had asked, 'I know this is very ignorant of me, but what exactly *is* a P.A. Maggy?'

'A P.A. is a production assistant, honey.'

'Like a personal secretary?' Ashley had queried. 'I know these questions must sound stupid, but it's my first film and I don't know a thing!' She had taken a sip of the aromatic coffee and looked at her new friend over the rim of her cup.

'It's not stupid to ask questions,' Maggy had assured her, 'as a matter of fact a P.A. is a lot like a good secretary. Luc calls me his "good right hand". But he's such a doll to work for, I figure you'd *have* to be good around him.'

Ashley had noticed that Maggy seemed to mention Lucas a lot. Perhaps he meant more to her than just her boss. After all, he had taken that photo of Bobby, which must mean they had contact outside their work. And Maggy's image of him was so different from hers—'a doll to work for'—the only doll he reminded her of, was a voodoo doll.

'Have you worked for Mr Martineaux a lot?' she had enquired.

'Lucas, honey—call him Lucas. Everyone on the set calls him that. I've been working for Luc since he started in this business. And Dan . . . that was my husband . . . worked for him too. Of course I work with other directors, but Luc's my favourite.'

Ashley had wondered if this remark was prompted by sentiment rather than professionalism. She had gone on probing.

'Why would you rather work for Mr Mar . . . er . . . Lucas, than any other director?'

Maggy had replaced her empty cup and signalled to the waitress for a refill. 'Because he's the best,' she had answered succinctly, 'also because he's the straightest, most decent boss you could wish for. You don't meet men like Lucas Martineaux very often.'

'You can say that again,' Ashley had agreed grimly. Encouraged by the other woman's openness, she then asked casually, 'Are you in love with him?'

Maggy had looked at her, wide-eyed, then thrown back her head and guffawed. 'In love? With Luc? Gee, you'd better not let my boy-friend hear you!'

And Ashley had joined in with her laughter, and idly

wondered why she should feel relief to learn that Maggy's relationship with their boss was not a romantic one.

Now, after nearly ten hours' sleep, she stood admiring the view from her floor-to-ceiling picture window, and marvelled that the central heating made it unnecessary for her to wear a dressing-gown over her nightie.

She consulted a folder titled 'Welcome To Toronto' that she had found on the bedside table. She realised that last night she had mistaken the dark blot of the Toronto Island as the far shore, instead of the heavily tree'd sand-bar, which boasted a yacht club, several beaches, and a children's amusement park and zoo during the summer months. The self-important ferry now ploughing across that stretch of slate cold water was the Island residents' connection with the Toronto mainland. Also the brochure informed her, there was a small airport on the western reaches of the Island. And sure enough, to her right she saw a tiny plane circle and prepare to land on the narrow runway set in barren snow-streaked fields.

There was a build-up of ice at the edges of the harbour, and a photograph showed the lake side of the Island in winter. On that side the ice was a massive green and white wall. For with nothing between Toronto and the USA, the inland sea was a vast sheet of water, sculpted at the shoreline into barbaric ice-forms by the fierce winds.

The strident jangle of the telephone broke into the stillness. She lifted the ivory-coloured receiver, so unlike the feel of a British phone. It was Maggy.

'Wakey-wakey, Ashley!'

'I've been awake for *ages*,' she protested. 'I'm standing here admiring the view.'

'Never mind the view. You'd better get a wiggle on, honey. Luc's picking you up to go to that costume fitting. He'll meet you in the lobby in fifteen minutes.'

'*Lucas* will?'

'Yeah! Said he's got to go there anyway, so he might as well take you, instead of getting a car and driver.'

'In fifteen minutes?' Ashley started shuffling off her nightdress while she talked.

'Yep! And he's *always* on time!'

'I'll be ready,' the now naked Ashley assured her. 'Bye!' She flung herself into the bathroom, gleaming with cream tiles and mirrors, and turned on the hot water for a shower. Hastily she pinned up her wealth of Titian hair and crammed it into a white plastic shower cap she found folded in a packet for the convenience of guests. The mirror, now pearled with steam, mistily reflected her slender white-skinned body.

Having hastily towelled herself dry on a thick brown bath towel the size of a small bedsheet, she pulled on grey wool culottes, her yellow sweater, and knee-high boots. She pulled a comb through her damp hair, touched her mouth with lip-gloss, and grabbing her winter coat and bag in one hand, hurried down to the main floor of the hotel.

He was waiting, leaning against the front desk talking to a lanky blond boy. He glanced briefly at Ashley, his piercing eyes taking in the damp tendrils of hair still clinging to her cheek, the trim culottes, the upward thrust of her breasts under the thick woollen sweater. She felt herself flush under his dispassionate scrutiny.

'Am I late?' She could have bitten out her tongue for making such a cowardly remark.

He glanced at the wafer-thin gold watch on his wrist. 'Very punctual. Full marks!' He turned to the blond young man. 'Tim, this is Ashley Morrison. Ashley, meet Tim Webber, our second A.D.'

The young man also appraised her, but his blue eyes were warm and friendly. 'Welcome to Canada, Ashley. Luc's told me a lot about you.'

'Oh dear!' she said, appalled.

Lucas ignored her. 'You'll see to the transportation snarl-up, then, will you, Tim? I want to be set-up at Tremblant by the end of the week.'

'Will do. We should be ready to roll day after to-morrow.'

'I'm counting on you, Tim,' Lucas nodded.

Dismissed, Tim left them with a brief smile for Ashley. Lucas uncoiled his lean frame from the desk. He was again wearing his jeans, topped by a pale blue crew-neck sweater and darker blue shirt. The colour set off his tanned skin and black unruly curls. He watched while Ashley struggled to put on her coat. Don't help me, will you? she thought bitterly. As if he could read her mind he put out a strong hand and proceeded to take her coat off again.

'Judging from the fact that your hair's still soaking wet I take it you've just come out of the shower,' he commented.

She faced him indignantly, her coat half on, half off. 'I showered ages ago.'

'Did you have any breakfast?'

'I don't eat breakfast, thank you,' she lied.

'Well, you'd better start. Filming's hard work, you need energy.'

'I'm not filming today. Just fittings.'

Exasperated, he yanked the coat from her shoulders. 'Do you have to contradict me all the time, Ashley? I'm trying to offer you a cup of coffee before we start, not a three-course meal.' He grasped her arm firmly and steered her towards the Quayside Lounge where he chose a table facing the high windows that looked out on to the lake. He seated himself on one of the velvet two-seater sofas. Ashley sat stiffly on the sofa opposite.

'A pot of coffee for two,' he said to the hovering waitress.

'I prefer tea,' said Ashley.

'Make that one coffee, one tea,' he smiled at the waitress, 'and some white toast for the lady.'

Ashley set her pretty mouth in an obstinate line. 'I'd like brown toast, please,' she said.

He raised his black brows in mock forbearance. 'Would you like anything to spread on it? Arsenic? Cyanide?'

In spite of herself, Ashley grinned. 'How about marmalade?'

'Brown toast with marmalade,' he said to the delighted waitress, 'and you'd better escape before the lady changes the order again.'

Ashley relaxed in her sofa and looked at him. His eyes had a rueful twinkle in them now, and he seemed less formidable. 'After all your lectures about the importance of breakfast are you only having coffee?' she asked.

'I breakfasted at the crack of dawn, young lady,' he said pleasantly enough, 'I had ham and eggs while you were still snoring your head off.'

'I don't snore!' She was quite indignant.

'I wouldn't know. Not having first-hand knowledge of your sleeping habits, which no doubt are enchanting,' he drawled. His sensual mouth tilted in a smile.

Ashley was suddenly intensely aware of his masculinity. She realised with a jolt that he was incredibly sexy. She noticed his lean, hard thighs in the tight jeans, the broadness of his shoulders. For a moment she had a crazy image of her naked self reflected in the steamy mirror upstairs, but this time it was Lucas who was drying her with the bath towel. His hands gentle . . . caressing . . . In horror at herself she slewed round in her seat and looked hard at the bitter cold water in an effort to regain her composure. She heard him chuckle softly.

'What a pretty view,' she remarked inanely, trying to distract his attention.

'Yes, Toronto has a pleasant lakefront.' He sounded amused, damn him.

'Ashley?' Reluctantly she tore her eyes from the scenery and faced him.

'Ashley, tell me, what is it about the lake that makes you blush?' He looked at her with fake innocence, and the tide of colour that had flooded her face heightened.

'I . . . I'm hungry!' she choked. 'I always blush when I'm hungry.'

'Well, I guess that's more attractive than having to listen to your tummy rumbling,' he answered chattily.

Mercifully the tea and toast arrived, and she ate and drank in silence, aware that he was watching her like a hawk, smiling his inscrutable mandarin smile.

They drove to the design studio in Lucas's car, a smart dark green Porsche, low-slung and smelling of leather. Ashley craned her neck, looking up at the glass skyscrapers that soared above the narrow streets. The glittering shops, the bustle and hum of the city. She noticed a large glass-domed building on one of the thoroughfares and asked him about it.

'That's the Eaton Centre,' he told her. 'There are something to the order of three hundred shops in that glass gallery. With your track record of extravagance I'd advise you to steer clear of it.'

Ashley bit her lip. It was difficult not to tell him that if he hadn't insisted on tea and toast this morning, she would have gone breakfastless in the interests of economy.

They drove past the Toronto City Hall, its twin clam-shell design like two curved hands. Skaters whirled on the frozen reflecting pool. Chestnut vendors peddled their wares.

The fitting was in Yorkville, a chic grid of streets, part of the original village of York, which was Toronto's name in its early history. The old houses had been renovated into smart shops and cafés, the sidewalks planted with trees, their bare winter branches etched against a pewter sky.

The design studio that was doing the costumes for the film was one of a sandblasted row of brick villas. The door was painted shiny black, and a single shining brass plate announced—'Desmond Designs'. Lucas ushered her into the hall—more sandblasted brick, spanking white paint and deep grey carpets. Modern, brightly coloured lithographs hung on one spotlit wall. They went through a door and entered the workroom. Here there was a violent contrast with the lush polished entrance. Things were shabby and chaotic—cutting tables, dressmakers' dummies, bales of fabric on shelves that lined the room, boxes of pins, tailors' chalk, and rack upon rack of period costumes labelled with scene numbers and actors' names. Several women were working at industrial sewing machines.

A middle-aged man wearing an enormous pair of horn-rimmed glasses materialised from behind a rack. He looked like a startled owl.

'Lucas!' he hooted. 'You're on time—what a blessing! I simply don't know how I'm going to get done today. I'm positively *panic-stricken*!' He waved his hands around in despair and stared at Ashley through his glasses.

'Relax, Desmond,' said Lucas. 'This is Ashley Morrison. Ashley, I'd like you to meet our designer, Desmond, one of the best in the business.'

'*Brute!*' Desmond squealed. 'You know very well I'm *the* best!'

'If you say so,' Lucas agreed curtly. Ashley detected a hint of distaste in his manner, and she wondered if, like her, he found such affected behaviour embarrassing. 'Now we've only got an hour, Desmond, so let's get on with it.'

Desmond dramatically examined Ashley from head to toe. '*Stunning!*' he breathed. 'Lucas, I congratulate you. She's absolutely stunning. She'll make a *divine* Elizabeth!'

'That remains to be seen,' said Lucas, 'but she should photograph well enough.' His brows were gathered into an irritated frown.

'Where can I change, Mr . . . er . . . Desmond?' Ashley broke in. She wasn't enjoying standing there being discussed by the two men as if she was one of the dressmakers' dummies.

With much twittering and hand-waving Desmond ushered her into a curtained-off corner of the untidy room.

'Strip off, darling,' he said. 'I'll get Maria to bring you your corset, then we'll try the ball-gown.'

Ashley was laced into a boned corset, several petticoats were dropped over her rufous head, and the ball-gown was produced. It was exquisite. Fashioned from pink silk, as pale as the heart of a rose, it was embroidered in gold thread with garlands of oak leaves. A froth of fine lace trimmed the three-quarter sleeves, and when she moved an under petticoat of aqua-coloured taffeta whispered faintly.

Desmond drew back the curtains with a flourish and chivvied her out to where Lucas was straddling a chair, leaning on the back of it, an enigmatic expression on his high-cheekboned face.

'Do you think the décolletage is low enough, Lucas?' Desmond asked, indicating Ashley's breasts with a careless gesture.

Lucas stared speculatively at the gentle curve of her white skin. She felt her cheeks grow hot, and fought the urge to cross her hands over her bosom to protect herself from his insolent gaze.

'I think it could be a bit lower,' he said finally. 'She's got a good figure, 'we might as well make the most of it.'

'Your pound of flesh?' Ashley snapped. If the ground had opened up and swallowed Lucas, she would have danced with joy. She suspected he was deliberately trying to humiliate her, to pay her back for her original snub. Well, she was damned if she was going to take it lying down! She'd let him know she recognised his tactics—recognised, and despised them.

'They wore their formal gowns cut low in those days,' Lucas explained, 'and I was paying you a compliment. No need to look like a bad-tempered porcupine.' He turned to Desmond who was standing by listening avidly to this exchange. 'Apart from the neckline the dress is fine. Now let's get on. I've got a busy day.'

The remainder of Ashley's wardrobe consisted of heavy serge skirts, blouses, and woollen shawls. She was fitted with laced boots, mittens, and a shabby black bonnet. An apron made out of sacking was provided.

'I don't want her in any kind of corset for the final scenes,' said Lucas. 'By that time she should look dirty and thin and poor.'

'Those costumes have all been made too large,' Desmond replied, 'and when they're broken down she'll look quite shapeless.' Ashley knew that 'broken down' was the theatrical term for making the costumes worn and dirty. 'Also we could bind her flat for those scenes,

Lucas,' Desmond suggested, 'that should help to make
her look thinner.'

Lucas nodded enthusiastically. 'Terrific idea. We'll do
that.' Ashley could have sworn he was gloating over the
discomfort this would cause her. 'Now get dressed,
Ashley. I'll just have time to drop you off at the hotel
before I go to the airport to meet Sloane.'

'Please don't trouble yourself about me,' she said
grandly, 'I'll find my own way back. Anyway, I have a
make-up appointment this afternoon, so I might as well
stay in town till then.'

'Make-up's the other side of town,' Lucas pointed out.

'I'm quite capable of finding my way!' She glared at
him defiantly.

'The taxi fare's pretty fierce from here . . . but that's
your business.'

'Exactly!'

'Well, don't get lost and don't be late.' He was mad-
dening! 'Ciao, Desmond. Nice work, tell you staff I said
so.' He waved an airy hand and was gone.

After Lucas left Desmond apparently discovered that
she existed and chatted away, exclaiming keenly over
her own clothes. Her culottes excited special comment.
But she was too aggrieved by Lucas's high-handed attitude to pay him too much attention, and she escaped as
soon as she could.

She explored Yorkville for a while, found a bank and
deposited her per diem money, and sent the bulk of it off
to England. This left her rather short of cash, and she
decided Yorkville was too expensive for lunch, so she
made her way to the nearest subway station and found
out how to get to her next appointment.

She had to change trains and then take one of Toronto's streetcars. She enjoyed the streetcar trip. It was
slow, but the clanging bell and lurching car was a novel-
ty. It was also an excellent way to sightsee. This part of
Toronto wasn't fashionable, but there were signs of the
renovation boom that had hit the city. Some of the
shabby streets were dotted with freshly painted and
scrubbed houses, usually sporting large wooden or brass

numerals, their windows crammed with plants, and the small front yards filled with chipped stone and empty flower boxes waiting for the spring planting.

Ashley had time to eat a hot-dog and a cup of coffee at a nearby 'greasy spoon' before going to her next appointment, which was in a gloomy six-storied building resembling a gaol. She was directed upstairs to the make-up department by a uniformed guard, and after some difficulty in the bewildering maze of corridors she knocked at the right door and went in.

Two women were standing by the brightly-lit mirrors that ran the whole length of one wall. One of the women was about forty; the other scarcely older than Ashley.

'You're Ashley Morrison—I recognise you from your photograph,' said the younger girl. She spoke with an English accent. 'My name's Jane, and I'm doing your make-up. And this is Claire,' she indicated her older companion, who smiled at Ashley and said a brief 'hello'. 'Claire will be doing your hair.' She glanced at her watch. 'Luc should be here any minute,' she said. 'Would you like a cup of coffee while we wait for him?'

Ashley refused the coffee and checked the time with the girl called Jane. 'I make it three,' she said, 'or is my watch fast?' She knew very well it wasn't, and she secretly exulted that she was on time and Lucas was the one who was late. Perhaps that would take him down a peg or two. 'Is Lucas often late?' she asked innocently, her grey eyes wide.

'He's on the dot usually,' said Jane. 'I can't think what's keeping him.'

'I can.' The woman called Claire spoke. 'Isn't Sloane Sheppard arriving today?'

Jane nodded knowingly. 'Of course! And time passes so quickly when you're with the one you love,' she crooned. 'I guess our Luc's forgotten about us in the excitement of seeing Sloane again.'

Ashley pricked up her ears. 'Are Lucas and Sloane Sheppard old friends, then?' Jane went into a fit of giggles. Claire answered.

'You could call them old friends, I guess. They were engaged at one time, but something went wrong, and the engagement was called off.'

'That's about ten years ago,' said Jane.

Claire corrected her. 'It's eight years ago, my dear.'

'I wouldn't know really,' the English girl said carelessly, 'I've only been in this country two years myself.'

'Well, *I* know,' said Claire. 'I was working with them when it happened. Luc was a first A.D. then, and Sloane was just beginning to get a name. I'll never forget it, because it's the only time I've found working with Luc difficult. He was like a bear with a sore head during the whole shoot.'

'Brokenhearted, poor lamb,' Jane said maliciously. 'And from what I hear he's been carrying a torch ever since.'

'Well, he hasn't been carrying it alone,' Claire commented drily. 'I've never known a man with as many women in tow as Lucas Martineaux.'

'And who can blame them?' purred Jane. 'He's a glorious hunk of man!' She picked up an eye-liner and examined the point. 'Isn't he?' she asked Ashley.

Ashley, who was trying to come to terms with the image of Lucas with a bevy of women in tow, didn't answer right away, and Jane repeated her question.

'Don't you think Luc's a glorious hunk of man?'

'He's attractive, I suppose,' Ashley said quietly. She was beginning to dislike this girl; her mindless gossip about Lucas got on her nerves.

'That's a very laid-back answer, I must say,' Jane turned to Claire. 'Don't you think that's very laid-back of Ashley?'

'Maybe it's just discreet,' the older woman said. 'We shouldn't tell tales out of school. Let's change the subject . . . Is your hair naturally curly, Ashley? Or is it permed?'

Ashley was grateful for the older woman's tact. She disliked gossip, and gossip about Lucas disturbed her in a way she couldn't fathom. The image of him bowling women over like ninepins was distasteful in the extreme.

It was a relief to talk of practical things and push thoughts of Lucas and his shadowy love-life to the back of her mind.

He arrived at last, fifteen minutes late and obviously annoyed.

'Sorry, everybody,' he said, 'Sloane's plane was late, and the traffic was heavy.' Ashley saw a look of complicity pass between Jane and Claire and she felt a stab of irritation. She wondered why on earth Sloane Sheppard couldn't have made her own way from the airport. Perhaps all that gossip about them was based on truth after all.

'Let's make a start,' said Lucas. Jane indicated the high make-up chair. Ashley clambered into it and Jane pinned her heavy curly hair off her face.

Lucas leaned over her, staring intensely into her face. His proximity was overpowering. She could see the texture of his brown smooth skin. His hair smelt like sweet warm grass.

'Now, Jane,' he said, 'I want the minimum of make-up. And above all don't blot out her freckles. I want to maintain the luminous quality of her complexion.'

Ashley felt weak with happiness. In spite of her hated freckles he liked her complexion.

'It'll film particularly well in the scenes where she's dirty.'

Her happiness left her, like air being let out of a balloon.

'I think just the eyes need make-up, really,' said Jane. 'She's got such smashing eyelids to work with. You've got wonderful eyelids, Ashley,' she nodded at Ashley in the mirror. 'Hasn't she got smashing eyelids, Luc?'

'Mmm.' He was noncommittal. Obviously her eyelids left him cold.

Now Claire joined the conference. Ashley's hair was unbound and brushed loose over her shoulders. It was decided that, apart from the earlier scenes, her hair would be either worn in a heavy braid, or left loose.

'And I want it dirty for the final scenes, so don't wash it for a few days,' Lucas ordered.

'Those scenes aren't till the end of the film,' Ashley pointed out.

'I'm not shooting in sequence,' he replied scathingly, 'this isn't a play. So I'd appreciate it if you conquered your natural actress's vanity for the sake of the film. I want your hair a mess, so *don't wash it*! Understood?'

'Understood,' she answered levelly. And although she felt her cheeks grow pink with mortification, her green gaze didn't waver, and he was the first to look away.

When the session was finally over, and she was brushing out her glossy chestnut mane, Lucas offered her a lift back to the hotel. 'Or do you still prefer to travel alone?' he asked. 'I warn you, you'll be caught in the middle of the rush-hour.'

Ashley had the feeling he was offering her an olive branch after his harsh behaviour, and with a final sweep of the hairbrush she accepted. To her surprise he reached out his hand and stroked her gleaming hair where it lay like a silk cape on her shoulders. At his touch, which was light as thistledown, her heart started to beat painfully fast, and a wild unexplainable elation flooded her. She felt his fingers tremble. He snatched his hand away as if it had been burnt and said gruffly:

'Don't let me ever catch you changing the colour of your hair . . . it's a glorious shade for film.'

She should have guessed his uncharacteristic gentleness was connected with his wretched filming! It had nothing to do with *her*. The unfamiliar elation deserted her and dully she put on her coat and followed him to the car.

The drive back was slow. It was dark now, and a few snowflakes were falling. The streets were choked with traffic, and crowds of returning office workers, their shoulders hunched against the raw wind that blew across the lake, scurried for the subway entrances, or huddled by the streetcar stops.

The car inched its way down Bay Street. Lucas was silent. He had taken off his leather driving gloves and his strong bare hands lay lightly on the black steering-wheel. While they waited at a red light he turned to Ashley.

'I didn't mean to put you down back there,' he said, 'about shooting out of sequence. Of course you couldn't know that. Besides, I haven't given out a schedule yet.' He flashed his gypsy smile. 'Bear with me, Ashley. It's been a difficult day.'

She discovered that when he smiled at her like that it was impossible to stay angry with him, and she smiled back. The traffic lights highlighted the dimple at the corner of her mouth.

'Forget it!' she shrugged. 'I'm woefully ignorant about film making. Do you always shoot that way? Out of sequence, I mean?'

'Well, filming isn't just a case of putting a story on to tape,' he replied. The light had turned green and now he was peering at the tail-lights of the car ahead, a web of fine lines marking the corners of his eyes. 'That would be easy. For this film, for instance, I need bad weather . . . for those final dramatic scenes where you're stranded deep in the bush. We'll be shooting in Tremblant Park in Quebec. It's very wild there, and has the sort of terrain we need. But we also need lots of snow . . . lots of it. If I shot the film in proper order we wouldn't get to Tremblant till March or April, and I can't bank on some really heavy blizzards in March the way I can in February . . . so we shoot the final scenes first. Also I can't get into the Casa Loma till March.'

'Get in where?'

'The Casa Loma. It's a copy of a mediaeval castle right in the middle of Toronto. It's all towers and turrets—a fantastic place. An Edwardian financier built it in 1911. Now it's open to the public, and also film companies and the likes of the Canadian Broadcasting Corporation rent it. It's a boon when you're making a period film.'

'All this chopping and changing from one part of the script to another must take a lot of concentration on the actors' part,' Ashley observed.

'On everybody's part,' he corrected her. 'Continuity is the name of the game—the emotion the character is portraying, the way the scene is shot. For instance, if an actor was drinking a glass of wine in one scene, and we return to finish that part several days later, the wine has to be at the same level in the glass, and the actor has to be holding it the same way. His voice and tone must match the previous scene. His emotional pitch must be the same. That's why I get mad when some people . . .' he gave her an oblique look, 'some people say filming's easy. Take it from me, it's *not*.'

'Have you ever worked in the theatre?' she asked.

'Ah! Your beloved theatre again.' He stabbed the accelerator and shot away from a stop light. 'As a matter of fact I have. It many surprise you to know I've directed several stage plays, but unlike you, I'm not a theatrical bigot.'

'I'm not a bigot!' she cried, hurt by his sudden attack.

'No? You sure behave like one.' She didn't answer, and after a silence he said, 'I told you this had been a difficult day, for God's sake don't add to it by sulking.'

Oh dear, thought Ashley, is he going to hop around from one mood to another like this when we're working?

'There are aspects of this business that I *loathe*,' Lucas went on bitterly. 'I detest the phoneyness, the . . . theatricality some people indulge in.'

'Do you mean me?' Her voice was tight.

'And the *self-centredness* of actresses,' he said unfairly, 'No, I *don't* mean you, as a matter of fact. So far you seem to behave quite normally. I was thinking of the beginning of my day, of Desmond posturing around his studio.'

'Desmond isn't an actor,' she pointed out reasonably.

He snapped back, 'Well, he behaved like one—throwing "darlings" around like confetti. It sets my teeth on edge!'

'Why are you in show business, then?'

'Because I love making films. I love the precision . . . the *truth* . . . of film-making. Your ball-gown, for instance,' he turned to regard her briefly before focusing his attention again on the slow-moving line of traffic, 'your ball-gown is made of silk—the authentic material of the period—because you can't lie to the camera. Nylon will not photograph the same. A canvas door won't sound right on a film set. The . . . the artificiality of the stage, the fake props, all perfectly acceptable when you have three feet of space between you and your audience—won't stand up under the eye of the camera. The same goes for performances. If the actor isn't totally truthful the camera will pick up the dishonesty of that performance, and the balance of the scene will be destroyed.'

His voice vibrated with enthusiasm. It was clear he was utterly dedicated to his profession.

'What is it you dislike about your work, then?' asked Ashley.

'Some of the people I have to work with. Oh, not the crew! Crews are made up of technicians, craftsmen and women. Real people, people without illusions of grandeur. They haven't time for phoneyness—not like a bunch of actors. Most of the trouble I run into on the set is caused by the conceited posturing of actors. And actresses. *Particularly* actresses,' he added bitterly.

'Since you have such a poor opinion of us I'm surprised you don't just make animal films,' Ashley said sweetly, looking at his profile through lowered lids.

He turned to her. 'Touché,' he said. 'You're a necessary evil, the bunch of you.'

'And you called *me* a bigot! I think that's a case of the pot calling the kettle black,' she smiled innocently.

Lucas sighed. 'True. Perfectly true, and perfectly just,' he said, 'don't confuse me, Ashley. I'm not used to dealing with reasonable actresses.'

'You have a terrible opinion of actresses!'

'I've had a lot of experience,' he muttered darkly, 'and all of it bad.'

After this exchange he relapsed into a gloomy silence, and Ashley was left to her own thoughts. She could only conclude that seeing Sloane Sheppard again must have upset him, and this had brought about his irrational attack on actresses in general.

For some reason the idea of Lucas and Sloane emotionally entangled discomfited Ashley, and it did no good her telling herself that it had nothing whatever to do with her, or that she couldn't care less. Because quite obviously, in some obscure part of her she did care, otherwise she wouldn't be disturbed. She had to admit she was beginning to enjoy his company. He irritated—yes, whipped her to fury at times. But hatred was no longer the emotion he inspired. She wasn't sure *what* emotion it was that had replaced her former antipathy, but she sensed that it was very potent, and that she was powerless to control it.

In spite of the warmth in the little car she shivered, and a feeling of delicious anticipation swept over her. Anticipation mingled with dread. For she had the distinct impression that she was standing on the brink of something momentous. That her life would never be quite the same again, and that no matter what the future held for her, there was no turning back.

CHAPTER FOUR

BACK in her room the red message light on her telephone was flashing. There were two messages, both of them from Maggy—one to let her know that the cast and crew would be leaving for Mont Tremblant in the morning, and the second an invitation for cocktails with the cast and crew to greet Sloane Sheppard.

A party to greet Sloane! That meant that the famous film star would be there in all her glory . . . with Lucas! Ashley pushed back the sliding door of her walk-in closet and reviewed her wardrobe. What she wore for this occasion was very important. She *had* to look her best, so that Lucas would still notice her, even when he was in the company of the dazzling Sloane.

Logic told her she was being ridiculous, that she was just a member of the cast, not important to him or to anyone else. Furthermore, that it didn't matter to her whether he noticed her at the party or not. But another part of her refused to listen to this reasonable voice, and her slim hands shook while she sorted through the evening wear Auntie Con had insisted making. She sent out a silent prayer of thanks to her aunt now, as she held each creation against herself, checking her reflection in the mirror.

After much agonising she finally settled on a jumpsuit made of silver material originally intended for making parachutes, and bought at a warehouse sale by her clever aunt years ago. The style was a copy of a French model that Ashley had admired in *Vogue*. Aunt Constance had cut out a pattern using that morning's paper, and whipped it up for her niece. Ashley's mother had donated an old silver belt that had once belonged to her grandmother. It was far too small for most people, but it just fitted Ashley. After a good polish it handsomely circled her slim waist, emphasising her fragility. The dull silver fabric gleamed in the light and clung to Ashley's lissom body like another skin.

She had time, so she piled her hair high, and wound it intricately round her head in a series of braids and loops. Tendrils, glinting red-gold, framed her temples and the tender back of her neck. She made up her eyes with care, brushing her thick lashes with mascara till they curled like the petals of a flower. She added a hint of blusher, and some coral lipstick to her well defined lips, then putting on her high-heeled silver sandals she pirouetted in front of the mirror, a slender silver spear, crowned with fire. She was glad the party was in the hotel, that meant she didn't have to wear her thick tweed overcoat, which certainly didn't go over her jump-suit. And silver strap sandals weren't ideal footwear for slushing through snow.

Pier Three was one of several large banqueting halls. Ashley's silver heels dug into thick cinnamon broadloom that carpeted the hall. The massive oak door muted the sounds of the party. Before she walked in she pulled down the front zipper of her jump-suit another half inch. Might as well play the role of glamour girl to the hilt! With beating heart she opened the door and made her entrance. The heavy door swung shut behind her, creating a dark backdrop.

She observed about fifty people scattered around the teak-walled room. Most of them were clustered round the bar, beside which was a table laden with cocktail goodies. Then she noticed that everyone was informally dressed. Jeans and shirts were the uniform. In her gleaming silver finery she stood out like a chandelier in a coalmine! Well, it was too late to turn back now. She would just have to carry it off with élan. She tilted her chin higher and walked determinedly towards the bar.

Maggy, heavy boots over her workaday jeans, detached herself from a group and came towards her.

'Hi, Ashley! Come and meet some of the people you'll be working with for the next few weeks.'

Dear Maggy! Not by a flicker of an eyelash did she betray the fact that Ashley was preposterously overdressed for this casual get-together of colleagues. Ashley could have kissed her.

She was introduced to a nice, fatherly man who, she was told, was 'chief grip'—a title she learned applied to the man who carried the tripod, adjusted the 'flags' on the lights, and was generally a jack of all trades, and worth his weight in gold on any film set. She met the 'gaffer' (chief electrician), the cameraman, who was originally from Yugoslavia, the sound man, a burly Scot, and the character actors who would be playing her parents in the film. The latter had both emigrated to Canada years before. They welcomed Ashley warmly, got her a glass of wine, and launched into a reminiscence about the 'good old days' of British theatre. Suddenly there was a stir and all eyes turned to the entrance.

The door had opened and Lucas was ushering in the most stunningly beautiful woman Ashley had ever seen. She was instantly recognisable. It was Sloane Sheppard. That oval face and luscious figure had been seen on countless television and film screens. Her raven black hair hung to her waist, straight and shining. Her eyes were light brown and dramatically made up, as was her sensual crimson mouth. She too wore jeans, expensive designer ones that clung to her long legs like silk stockings. As she undulated into the room—for she didn't walk like ordinary mortals—she shrugged off her short fur jacket, revealing a scarlet turtle-necked sweater that moulded her full breasts, and set off a narrow gold belt drawn tightly round her waist. An aura of sexuality surrounded her like perfume.

Ashley fought the desire to hide herself behind the two character actors and zip up her jump-suit. She prayed that the moment she had been introduced she could remove her overdressed self without being missed. With this end in view she inched away from the bar area, hoping to remain unobtrusive, hoping her glinting silver finery was overshadowed by the dazzle of this gorgeous sex-goddess who clung so possessively to Lucas's arm. But it was no good. He caught sight of her immediately and cut off all escape. He had changed his blue jeans for supple beige suede slacks and jacket, which he wore with casual elegance.

Ashley forced herself not to colour when Lucas's derisive eyes raked her silver-clad form from throat to ankle. He introduced the famous actress, who looked searchingly at the discomfited girl.

'What have you been up to, Ashley?' he drawled. 'Making a commercial for the Silver Bullet?'

In spite of her efforts the dreaded rosy flush swept over Ashley's cheeks, but before she had a chance to reply Sloane Sheppard spoke.

'Pay no attention to him, Ashley. He's just the *rudest* thing!' She turned a melting brown eye on Lucas. 'She looks absolutely adorable, Lucas Martineaux, and you *know* it,' she purred. She focused the full battery of her charm on Ashley. 'I just wish I owned a lovely . . . costume . . . like that. *I'd* wear it all the time too, believe me!'

Her brown-eyed stare was blank, but Ashley could have sworn there was an edge of bitchiness in the husky voice that ran from satin to sandpaper.

'I do take it off to go to sleep,' Ashley said, and heard Lucas give a strangled chuckle.

'Really?' Sloane fluted. 'I would have thought it would have looked *stunning* in *bed*.' She smiled, her eyes as cold as brown glass.

Sensing battle, Ashley was about to answer this when Tim Webber joined them.

'Ashley,' he crowed, 'how great that you're here! You look just terrific!' He glowed at her, and turned to Lucas. 'Doesn't she look terrific?' he said. 'Quite the most beautiful thing in the room.'

Sloane pushed herself forward. 'Thank you, Tim,' she said coldly.

Tim turned beet-red. 'Sloane, I . . . I didn't notice you . . . that is . . .'

The beautiful brunette gave him a withering stare. 'You haven't changed,' she said, 'you always did have an eye for the obvious.' She cast a jaundiced look at Ashley, then turned her attention to Lucas, her full crimson mouth drooping discontentedly. 'Luc, I want to leave,' she pouted. 'Let's go on to the Martins' bash. It'll be more lively there.'

Lucas removed Sloane's red-tipped hand from his arm. 'This party was organised in order for you to meet the other members of the cast and crew,' he said firmly. 'I expect you to have the courtesy to stay and mingle for a while before taking off for your jet-set friends.' He spoke quietly, but there was no denying the authority in his tone. Ashley and Tim waited with bated breath to see how the sultry movie queen would react.

Sloane's tortoiseshell-coloured eyes narrowed, then she made a moue. 'Well, all *right*,' she said grudgingly, 'we can go on to the Martins' later.'

'*You* can go on later,' Lucas replied. 'I dislike them and their style of parties.'

'Let's not discuss it in front of the hired help,' Sloane looked disdainfully at Ashley. 'If I have to stay, at least you can get me a drink.'

'Of course. And what about you, Ashley?' asked Lucas. 'Would you like another glass of wine?'

'No, thank you.' Ashley decided to remove herself. Her presence seemed to be irritating the glamorous star. 'I have to be going now. I . . . I have to . . . go out to dinner.'

'Gee, I was going to ask you to have dinner with me,' said Tim, looking quite put out.

Lucas looked put out too, which didn't make sense. 'I didn't know you had friends in Toronto,' he said.

Ashley made enigmatic noises and put her empty glass down on one of the low tables.

'Well,' said Tim, 'when we get to Tremblant you must have dinner with me there.'

'She'll be too busy to go out on dates at Tremblant,' Lucas said. He sounded annoyed. Ashley glared at him.

'That would be lovely, Tim,' she was sweet as honey, 'I shall look forward to it. Goodnight, Miss Sheppard. I'm very excited to have the opportunity to be working with you,' she added sincerely, 'I admire your talent very much.' The dark-haired star thawed considerably and bade Ashley a reasonably pleasant goodnight.

Pointedly ignoring Lucas, Ashley left the party and went back to her room. She was so hungry she could have eaten toothpaste!

She checked her money and decided that she didn't have enough for a proper meal, certainly not in one of the hotel restaurants. She had planned to fill up on the cocktail snacks provided, but the encounter with Sloane and Lucas had put paid to that. Besides, she could hardly gorge herself on titbits if she was supposed to be dining out. She remembered seeing a twenty-four-hour shop called 'Mac's Milk' in the shopping concourse beneath the hotel, and pulling on her winter coat to cover her suit she made her way downstairs.

She bought a small jar of peanut butter, a packet of crackers, and a carton of chocolate milk. She had noticed some benches along the walls near the shop and decided to picnic there rather than in her room. She didn't want to risk bumping into someone like Tim in the elevator. And the place was deserted, she could eat her makeshift meal in peace.

She solved the problem of getting the peanut butter out of the jar with the handle of her nail file and happily started on her feast.

She was just in the process of piling peanut butter on to her second biscuit when Lucas turned the corner at a brisk pace. Ashley sat frozen for a couple of seconds, her peanut butter-laden nail file poised.

He stopped dead, then came towards her. 'I thought you were going out to eat?' he said.

'I am out,' she said as she finished spreading the cracker.

He stared at her accusingly. 'You said you had a date for dinner.'

'I didn't. You assumed I had a date.' She bit off the end of the crisp biscuit with her pretty white teeth.

'Is that your dinner?'

Her mouth was full, so she merely nodded vigorously, shaking loose a silken auburn curl.

'Honestly, Ashley! You try me beyond endurance!' he exclaimed, his square brow creased with exasperation.

She swallowed and looked at him mildly. 'Why?'

'Because what you're eating is a *picnic*, and you need proper meals. You don't seem to realise the kind of energy you're going to need for this job.'

'You sound like Auntie Con,' she said, and took a swig of chocolate milk.

'I don't know who Auntie Con is, but she sounds like a sensible person. No doubt you drive her to distraction too.'

'Anyway, what are you doing down here, sneaking around corners?' Ashley asked, setting down her milk carton, 'I thought you were going to a party with Miss Sheppard.'

'I skipped it.' Lucas sounded pleased with himself. 'I sent her off with Tim—do them both good. And for your information, I'm not sneaking around corners, I came down to buy some ice-cream. I live here, remember?'

'Ah yes!' Ashley dug her nail file into the peanut butter again.

'For heaven's sake stop stuffing yourself with that muck!' He took the jar from her and screwed the lid back on. 'I've enough steak for two. I'll feed you dinner.'

Ashley was hungry, and steak sounded wonderful. Nevertheless she refused. 'No, thank you, I'm . . .'

'Shut up and stop arguing!' he barked imperiously, yanking her to her feet. 'Come and help me choose the ice-cream.' He dragged her, protesting, into the store.

He bought *two* kinds, since she refused to help him choose. 'Double chocolate for me because I love chocolate,' he said, 'and pistachio for you because it matches your mean green eyes.' For indeed, Ashley's eyes had turned glass-green with indignation at his high-handed treatment.

He tucked the ice-cream under one arm and held her firmly with the other. 'Come on!' he said, pulling her unceremoniously to the hotel lobby. 'Come on—I'm starving!'

'I'm not,' she fibbed, but he paid no attention.

He hauled her across the glassed-in walkway that connected the hotel to the apartments, up the express elevator to his penthouse apartment, and opening the heavy wooden front door—plain apart from a brass nameplate and a shiny doorknocker shaped like a lion's head—pushed her in ahead of him and switched on the lights.

The penthouse was on two levels. The entrance was on the upper one, and the kitchen, dining room, and living rooms were below. Like the rest of Harbour Castle, the wall facing the lake was entirely made of glass. Lucas's windows were framed in curtains of pale yellow silk which gave a cosiness to the large modern rooms and light-coloured walls.

'Take your coat off,' he said, 'and make yourself at home while I fix dinner.'

He slipped off her coat and for a second his fingers rested on her shoulders. A faint tingle ran through her at his touch.

'Would you like a drink?' She thought his voice sounded suddenly hoarse, and her own had a shake in it when she declined the offer.

'Well, I'm having one,' he said. 'There are magazines on the table. The evening paper . . .' He seemed as nervous as a short-order cook confronted with a banquet. Surely someone as controlled as Lucas Martineaux wouldn't be thrown off balance by the task of preparing a simple meal for two?

Ashley went into the sunken living-room. It was decorated in shades of yellow and cream. A thick cream rug, patterned with splashes of gold and lemon, lay on the gleaming hardwood floor. Two enormous deep sofas, upholstered in cream tweed and scattered with bright cushions, faced each other over an oval glass-topped coffee table. Teak shelves held a collection of exquisite jade figurines. A beautiful antelope head carved out of ebony stood on a sideboard. Another table held a collection of antique silver snuffboxes. There were several pictures. One she particularly liked was a modern lithograph, an arresting totem of colour, grey, blue, red, yellow, with a shocking pink crescent accenting it. There were some traditional watercolours, and an oil painting of a horse which looked as if it dated from the eighteenth century. There were books and magazines on an old pine table by the window, and plants in a variety of pots, some modern pottery, some antiques of brass and china, worn smooth with age.

It was an eclectic room, as full of surprises as its owner.

Ashley glanced over the books and magazines. Trade papers. A dictionary of the theatre. Autobiographies. Some whodunits. Dickens—Thackeray—Canadian novels . . . Margaret Lawrence, Hugh Garner. Poetry (a surprise, that), again a mixture—Tennyson, Margaret Atwood, T. S. Eliot. A volume of Shakespeare's plays lay open at *King Lear*. Some books in French were stacked on a special shelf.

Lucas poked his head out of the kitchen. 'How do you like your steak?' he asked. 'I like mine rare.'

'I like *mine* medium,' she answered.

'That figures!' He grinned his boyish smile and disappeared into the kitchen again. 'Do you think we'll ever agree on anything, Ashley?' he raised his voice to ask.

'Maybe not on steak, but certainly on literature, Lucas.' She went to the kitchen entrance and held up one of his books. 'This, for instance—it's fascinating!'

Fork in hand, he turned from the stove to look at her choice. '*The Origins and History of Canadian Indians*,' he read aloud. 'That kind of stuff interests you, eh?' He looked inordinately pleased.

She flushed with enthusiasm. 'Oh yes! I love reading about other cultures. While I'm here I want to find out as much about this country and its people as I can.'

'There are times when I wonder if you're an actress at all, young lady,' he observed.

'What do you mean?'

He arched one black brow. 'It's rare, Ashley Morrison—it's practically *impossible*, to meet any actress who's interested in anything outside of herself and her own narrow world. Most of them read the latest play, plus the entertainment section of the newspaper, and that's *it*! It makes for some pretty dull conversation, believe me.' He removed one steak from the broiler.

'I think you exaggerate, Lucas,' she replied, handing him a plate. 'Besides, actors should make it their business to be in touch with world events, otherwise how can they portray human situations on stage?'

'My point exactly,' Lucas nodded, 'but precious few of your colleagues bother.'

'Well, I think that's stupid.'

'That's the second time we've agreed in five minutes, Ashley,' he said, 'we'd better watch it. We're liable to wind up being friends.' But his eyes smouldered with something deeper than friendship. The blood came to her face, and her knees grew weak beneath her.

He turned back to check the stove and took out the second steak. 'Dinner's ready,' he said. 'Come and eat.'

They ate in the kitchen, sitting on white directors' chairs at a round white-topped formica table. There was a modern print on one wall, a still life of fruits and vegetables. Over the sink hung a child's crayon drawing of an apple tree, erratically printed—'LOVE TO UNCLE LUC', and scattered with a multitude of Xs.

They ate the thick juicy steaks with grilled tomatoes, a tossed green salad, and a dish of potato crisps. Lucas poured red wine into long-stemmed crystal goblets.

'I don't think I should have any wine,' Ashley told him. 'My jet-lag's beginning to catch up with me.' This was true, she was beginning to feel sleepy.

He overrode her objection. 'A glass of Beaujolais won't hurt you,' he insisted, 'you don't have to drive home.'

'I may fall asleep over my steak.'

'If you do I shall carry you to your room and put you to bed.' He lifted his glass, his eyes taunting her over the crystal rim. 'To you.' His gaze drifted frankly to the upward thrust of her firm young breasts, which were accentuated by the tight silver fabric stretched across them.

Involuntarily her hands flew to raise her zipper. She dropped them and blushed scarlet with embarrassment at this gaucherie. He laughed softly, raised his glass again, and took a sip of the dark red wine. His eyes never left her for a second.

'To us,' he said softly.

'No,' she corrected him, 'to the film. I think it has a better future.'

Lucas put down his glass. 'Such a pessimist!' he mocked. 'Relax, Ashley. I won't tuck you up in bed, I promise.'

'Good.'

'Not tonight, anyway.' His brazen eyes challenged, and the atmosphere between them crackled.

This brash technique, while it might delight Sloane Sheppard, and no doubt accounted for his success with other women, wasn't going to work with her! Her hands might be trembling and her senses reeling, but she was darned if she would let him know it.

Very deliberately she cut a morsel of the steak in front of her, examined it carefully and said:

'Lovely steak, Lucas. Cooked to a turn.'

There was a silence during which she waited for the storm to break, but to her relief he started laughing. The tension eased between them, and the dangerous moment had passed.

'You are too much, Ashley,' he shook his head, 'you are something else!'

'Would it be sacrilegious to ask for mustard?' She opened innocent eyes wide and took a sip of wine. It was like silk on her tongue.

'Hot mustard, no doubt?' he commented. 'To match your temper.' He handed her a jar of mustard and started eating his own dinner.

She enjoyed the meal. The steak was tender, the salad crisply flavoured with a hint of garlic, and the tomatoes were bursting, sugar-sweet, out of their thin skins.

After the ice-cream—Lucas had insisted she have a double scoop of both flavours—he served coffee in eggshell-thin china mugs, which they took into the living room.

Ashley sat demurely in one of the armchairs near the window. No lolling about on sofas near him! Too dangerous, she decided. He acknowledged her tactics with a lopsided smile, but said nothing, and after switching on the tape deck, settled himself indolently in a corner of the sofa nearest to her chair. Soft jazz piano music filtered into the room.

'Were you on the level about this?' He held up the copy of the book on Canadian Indians.

'I told you I was.'

'Here!' he handed her the book, 'keep it,' he insisted, 'I can pick up another copy any time.' Ashley took the heavy volume gratefully. 'I have a particular interest in native people myself,' Lucas volunteered.

'Because of the film?' *Time of Trial* dealt with the relationship of an Indian girl—played by Sloane Sheppard—and a family of English settlers.

'Not entirely. One of my ancestors married an Algonquin woman way back. So there's also Indian blood in my veins.'

That explained those high handsome cheekbones, she realised.

'Does that shock you?' Lucas sounded defensive.

'Is it supposed to?'

'Not necessarily. But you're so . . . so *English*. You might find it distasteful.'

She took a sip of the rich coffee, then nursed the dark brown mug in her slim hands. 'You do have the most extraordinary prejudices,' she observed. 'First actresses . . . now the English!'

He shrugged eloquent shoulders. 'I guess you're right. But you don't behave the way most actresses do . . . apart from your mindless extravagance, that is. It throws me.'

She decided to ignore this. 'Martineaux's a French name, isn't it?' She asked. 'Are you full-blooded French Canadian? Apart from the Algonquin ancestor, that is.'

'Oh no, I'm a real mongrel.' He stretched out his long

legs and she was aware of the muscles flexing along his
hard thighs. 'My mother was English from Vancouver,
she died some time ago. My father's third generation
French Canadian. All of us kids grew up speaking both
languages.'

'Do you come from a big family?' She wanted to
find out as much as she could about this enigmatic man
while the atmosphere between them was warm and
peaceful.

'Three of us. I have an older sister—married with two
kids—' (that explained the drawing in the kitchen), 'and
a younger brother at university.'

'You're the only one in the film business, then?'

'No one else is nuts enough.' He grinned at her and
she felt an inexplicable surge of happiness. It felt so
right, sitting here companionably with Lucas in this
warm room, while the cold Canadian winter pressed
against the windows, and the sound of the music mingled
with the fragrant scent of their coffee.

'My father's an art historian,' he informed her, 'and
my kid brother's studying to be a lawyer.'

'And your sister?'

'Marie-André's an interior designer. But she only
works part-time till the kids are older. She feels her
children come before her career . . . unlike most theatrical mothers, who seem to use their offspring for
publicity gimmicks.' He looked at her searchingly.
'Another of my prejudices, eh?'

'One of the things that worries me about being an
actress,' Ashley admitted, lulled into a sense of confidence by the cosy tête-à-tête that had gone on between them, 'is the pull between needing the . . . the
ordinary things, like a home and children . . . and the
need to act . . . to work.'

Lucas pulled himself tensely upright in his seat. 'That
shouldn't be a conflict,' he said. 'At our first meeting you
told me that you were "totally dedicated to the theatre"
Right?'

'Yes, but . . .'

'Well, work always wins the toss. The *ordinary* things,

as you call them, get sacrificed for the sake of the glamour, the surface glitter, of fame.'

'Not always, surely?' she ventured.

'Oh yes—always, surely,' he scoffed. 'Anyone who looks for a lasting, an *honest* relationship, in this business is a fool.'

His eyes were stony. It was as if he had deliberately shattered the relaxed ambience between them and drawn his former hostility around himself like armour, to protect him from . . . from *what*? Not from her, surely?

'That's a pretty bleak outlook,' she said.

'Bleak or not, it's reality,' he replied bitterly, 'as I know to my cost.'

'Just because you may have had an unfortunate experience there's no need to be so extreme.' She made a point of remaining calm—a stratagem which seemed to madden him even more.

However, before anything more could be said the telephone shrilled, adding its discordant note to the strained atmosphere. Lucas bounded across the room in two long-legged strides.

'Hello!' he barked. Whatever was said at the other end of the line clearly didn't please him, the cleft between his black brows deepened. 'I warned you it would be that kind of party, Sloane,' he said.

So the call was from Sloane Sheppard. It would seem the gossip in the make-up room this afternoon wasn't so idle after all. Sloane would hardly be phoning him so late if it were merely a working relationship between the star and her director.

'Isn't Tim still with you?' Lucas growled into the phone. Ashley could just hear the high-pitched gabbling coming from the other end of the line rise a decibel. 'Then why don't you take a cab?' he suggested ungallantly. 'It's not convenient to come and pick you up. I'm entertaining.'

Ashley stood up. 'I was just going, Lucas . . .'

'*Sit down!*' This was said so vehemently that she obeyed without a murmur. He turned his back and hissed into the phone, 'Now you listen to me, Sloane. I'm not going to drop everything and come out to get you. You will take a cab; you will charge it to the company; and you will stop behaving like a spoiled brat. *Goodnight!*'

He slammed down the receiver, turned round, and glared at Ashley as if it was all her fault. She glared right back.

'God protect me from actresses,' Lucas muttered through gritted teeth.

'He'll certainly protect you from this one if you'll allow me to leave now,' she remarked drily.

He took a deep breath and turned to look moodily through the windows at the lake where the wind-tossed lamps on the jetty made quivering golden reflections on the inky water.

'Damn Sloane anyway,' he muttered.

The last thing Ashley wanted was to listen to Lucas on the subject of Slaone Sheppard. It was manifestly clear to her now that she had only been invited to share his dinner because he'd quarrelled with the raven-haired movie star, and had been at a loose end. She had merely been a diversion. And his earlier sexual flirting had been his male ego idling away the time with a conquest or two before breakfast.

She stood again, and this time Lucas did not stop her.

'Thank you for dinner,' she said politely, though she sounded as frosty as the ice forming like lace on the windows.

He turned to face her, running his long fingers through his unruly black curls, making them untidier than ever. With a mocking bow he said: 'You are entirely welcome, Miss Morrison.' With great formality he handed her the crumpled brown paper bag containing the remnants of her peanut butter and crackers. Then he started to help her into her coat.

'Just a moment!' he said, turning back into the living room. 'You forgot this.' He held up the copy of the book he had given her. Ashley wasn't sure she wanted to

accept it now, but it seemed childish to refuse, so she
took it silently.

He insisted on walking her back across the walkway
to the hotel lobby, and after she had got her key from
the desk, took her arm and went to the elevator with
her.

'There's no need to come up with me, Lucas,' she said
in a sudden panic. But he merely tightened his hold on
her arm.

'I always see my date to her door,' he said. 'What sort
of clod do you take me for?'

'I'm hardly in the category of a date,' she pointed out.

He gave her a thin-lipped smile and remained silent
until they reached her room. He took the key from her
nerveless fingers and opened the door. She turned on the
threshold.

'Goodnight, Lucas,' she said firmly, 'thank you again
for dinner.'

'Not at all.' He stepped past her into the room. 'I'm
glad to see they've given you a decent place.' He sounded quite chatty.

'Yes.' Her voice was cool, but her heart was beating
like a trip hammer. 'And now, Lucas, you must go. I still
have to pack for tomorrow . . .'

'You can leave some stuff here at the hotel, you
know,' he said, 'no need to pack everything.'

'I know. And now goodnight, Lucas . . . I'm very
tired . . . jet-lag, and . . .'

She knew he was playing with her, teasing. He probably recognised her panic and was laughing at her. She
set her soft lips into a firm line. 'Goodnight, Lucas.'

He chuckled softly—a sexy, wicked sound. She
steeled herself for his kiss, her hands balled into fists
ready to fight him off. He leaned over her, so close she
could see the gold medallion lying against the black hair
on his chest. Her heart was beating such a wild tattoo she
felt sure he must hear it.

'Goodnight, little Ashley. Sleep well,' he whispered.

Her lips involuntarily relaxed for his kiss. He laughed
softly again and gently tilted her chin. Her lashes

drooped, fanning her cheeks, and she held her breath, waiting, waiting . . .

The door clicked shut and she was alone, eyes closed, hands clenched ready to defend herself, lips softly pouting for the kiss she had felt was inevitable. A kiss her good sense told her she must repulse—even if her treacherous mouth gave the lie to this resolve.

Lucas had deliberately humiliated her. He had somehow contrived to make her appear eager for his kisses, then left her standing like an idiot.

She gave a sob of fury and threw the brown paper bag across the room in a surge of rage. A shower of cracker crumbs scattered over the thick brown carpet, and the peanut butter jar rolled silently into a corner.

She started to put clothes into a suitcase, well aware that her fury was partly directed at herself. Because the truth was . . . she *had* wanted him to kiss her. At least, she had wanted him to *try*. She had wanted to feel his sensual mouth on hers for a moment before she pushed him away.

And he had sensed that. That was why he had laughed so confidentially . . . conceited brute! He had made another conquest as surely as if he had carried her off to bed; she would never forgive him, and she'd make sure never to put herself in that position again. No more tête-à-têtes with the boss, thank you very much. She'd learned her lesson!

When she put her head on the pillow she was still seething and sure she would be unable to sleep a wink. But youth and jet-lag overcame her, and she slept soundly in spite of her emotions, and woke next morning with her temper dulled but still smouldering.

This was the morning the company left for Mont Tremblant, Quebec. The arrangement was for them all to congregate in the lobby after breakfast. Since Ashley's cash situation was now becoming acute, she rescued her crackers and peanut butter and ate them in her room before joining the company for coffee downstairs.

There was an air of festivity among the actors involved

in the location shoot, and the baggage-strewn hotel lobby had a misleading air of the beginning of a winter holiday, rather than the start of some very hard work.

They were to travel in a caravan—three big trucks with light and sound equipment, followed by the 'winne-bagos'—small overnight camping vans, used as dressing and make-up rooms, plus a few hired station wagons. Ashley was to travel in the make-up winnebago with Claire and Jane.

Maggy and Tim, both bundled up in down-filled parkas, joined the group and started organising the luggage, and assigning seats in the various vehicles. Maggy caught Ashley's eye and gestured towards a particularly large pile of scarlet leather suitcases taking up a great deal of space in the lobby.

'Sloane's idea of travelling light!' she whispered. 'I may well kill her before this film's finished.'

'Is she having a lorry all for herself?' Ashley giggled. So far she'd counted twelve pieces, all with the gold monogram SS.'

'A what? Oh—truck, you mean.' Maggy's round face took on an expression of vexation. 'Haven't you heard?' she said. 'Sloane's far too grand to travel with *us*. She's persuaded Luc to drive her to Tremblant. It's a real pain. I was supposed to drive down with him, that way we could have got some work done en route. But no! Madame wants him all to herself—and what Sloane wants she gets.' She moved away, little guessing the ferment she had caused in Ashley with this information.

There must have been a grand reconciliation. No doubt Lucas had relented and gone to collect Sloane from her party after all. Right after he'd left Ashley standing like a fool waiting to be kissed.

He had won that round sure enough. Though why she should think of her relationship with him in terms of prize-fighting was obscure. Indeed, why should she care if Lucas and Sloane went to Tremblant by balloon?

But she wasn't about to face that question yet. She had an idea she wouldn't like the answer.

'Hey, beautiful! Come back to earth!'

Tim was standing in front of her staring at her pensive, delicately contoured face. She smiled at him.

'Sorry, Tim, I was miles away. Is it time to go?'

'Sure is. Listen, beautiful—I've had a neat idea. Why don't you drive to Tremblant with *me* instead of in the winnebago? I sure could use the company, and I can't think of nicer company than yours. What do you say?'

Why not? she thought. If Lucas could drive Sloane, why shouldn't she go with Tim?

'It sounds great, Tim,' she said, 'as long as Claire and Jane don't mind.'

'Heck, no! They've got each other for company, I'm all on my lonesome. We might even manage that dinner date.' He was like an eager puppy.

While he stowed her luggage in the winnebago—there was no room in his rented station wagon—Ashley allowed herself to feel a small thrill of triumph. This would show Lucas! For surely it would prove that she didn't give a hoot whether he kissed her or not. Somehow it would pay him back for his contemptible behaviour last night, and restore her own wounded pride. For she still burned with mortification at the memory of his soft laugh when he left her standing—chin raised, eyes closed—in anticipation of his kiss.

CHAPTER FIVE

FOR the entire drive to Mont Tremblant Ashley felt as if there were three people in the car. She and Tim—and Lucas. She simply couldn't get Lucas out of her mind. His presence was as tangible as if he'd been sitting there between them. She smiled and chatted with Tim, and admired the passing scenery, but the centre of her attention, the core of her, was obsessed with images of Lucas. She saw him again, boldly looking at her over his wine glass. She could almost conjure the scent of his warm flesh when he had tilted her chin and leaned down as if to kiss her, the gold chain glinting against the crisp hair on his chest; his mobile mouth curved in a mocking smile.

I'm falling in love with him! she thought, and panic swept over her at the idea of such a hopeless attachment.

'When we get to Gananoque we'll lose the rest of the caravan, take the scenic route.' Tim's voice broke into her reverie. 'You must get a glimpse of the Thousand Islands while you're in Canada.'

Ashley forced herself to appear enthusiastic. 'Yes, that would be lovely.'

'This part of the drive's kinda dull, but it improves later,' Tim told her.

'I don't find it dull,' she assured him, 'it's just that it's so *big*. So different from home.'

'You looked a bit glazed,' Tim remarked astutely, 'I thought highway 401 was getting you down.'

'Rubbish, Tim!' She banished the image of Lucas to the back of her mind and really concentrated on the view. 'I'm just not at my best in the morning, that's all.'

'Well, I hope for your sake you get used to mornings,' said Tim. 'Filming demands pretty early starts.'

'So I've heard. Don't worry, Tim, I'll adjust.' She

reflected that early mornings were the least of her problems.

The day was clear and sunny, the sky blue like an inverted blue bowl of ice arched over Lake Ontario, a limitless expanse of water, aptly named an 'inland sea'. It stretched, sparkling aquamarine under the cloudless sky, to the distant horizon. The country on their left was hilly, dotted with dark fir trees, like sentinels against the snow-covered hillsides. Sometimes a great bluff of weathered rock frowned down at the straight ribbon of highway, and dense forests of spruce crowded in the valleys below.

As he had promised Tim took the scenic route when the road branched at Gananoque, and he slowed down so she would have an opportunity to enjoy the panorama, which was spectacular.

The Thousand Islands lay in the St Lawrence river. They were pink granite and limestone, and were dotted across the broad ice-strewn water as if some giant had scattered a bag of pebbles at random. The islands were thickly covered with trees, some skeletal with winter, some dark evergreen. Many of the islands were big enough to contain several large houses. Some were so tiny they could barely support the ramshackle lean-to's built on them as duck-hunters' blinds or fishermen's huts. A few very large islands had stately mansions built on them. Bolt Castle was one. Never completed, it was now owned by the United States Government, and was a famous tourist attraction in the summer. It was Mr Bolt's personal chef who had invented and named the famous Thousand Islands salad dressing as a tribute to the place. The graceful International Bridge spanned the St Lawrence at the western end, a link to the United States which was on the further shore.

'This is a great place in the summer,' said Tim, 'the sailing's terrific, and the swimming. You can watch the Great Lakers going down the St Lawrence Seaway.'

'Great Lakers?'

'Huge grain carriers. At night they look like floating hotels with all the lights on.'

'Gananoque! It's such a funny name,' said Ashley.

'It's Indian. It means "land which slopes towards the water and disappears under it".'

'Goodness!' Ashley giggled. 'I can see why they've kept the Indian name. It's quite a mouthful in English.'

'Yeah! What do you say we stop here and stretch our legs, have some coffee? OK?'

'Fine.'

He was clearly trying to please her, to make this trip a pleasure. It wasn't his fault that compared to Lucas—even the *memory* of Lucas—he seemed insipid.

If I have to fall in love why can't I fall in love with Tim Webber? Ashley thought. He's a nice young man, much more suitable than Lucas. But she was sensible enough to know that love cannot be forced. It strikes at will.

They drank coffee in a café whose windows overlooked the surging river. Great chunks of ice sometimes floated by, making the water appear an even darker green by contrast.

She tried to keep her attention on Tim—he was going on at great length about his old university, which was at Kingston, a town they had passed further back—but her attention kept wandering. The truth was, Tim bored her. His company simply served to point out how stimulating it was being with Lucas, and how dull everything was when Lucas wasn't around.

With a pang she wondered if last night Lucas had contrasted her company this way with Sloane's, and found her wanting compared to the exotic star.

They climbed back into the car and she was silent most of the way to Montreal. They stopped there for a grilled cheese sandwich and a Coke. It was still sunny, but she was conscious of a distinct nip in the air, and there was more snow here than in Toronto. Tim pointed out the silhouette of Mont Royale, Montreal's famous mountain which stood in the centre of the city crowned with an illuminated cross. A cluster of suburbs around its lower slopes.

After their snack they turned north and drove towards

the Laurentians—the oldest mountains in the world—
mountains that had once been as high as the Alps, until
centuries of wind and glaciers had smoothed them into
rounded, wooded giants, slumbering now under their
winter blanket of snow.

The road dipped and climbed. Brightly painted ski
chalets clustered in the valleys. On the sides of many of
the mountains ski-trails cut a swathe through the trees,
and she could see miniature figures being towed up to
the snowy crests, then making their swift zig-zagging
descent across the face of the hill.

They drove on steadily towards Mont Tremblant, the
three-thousand-foot peak the Indians named 'Trembling Mountain' because it lies on a fault line and has a
history of tremors.

There were fewer houses now, and the scenery was
wilder. The primaeval tree-topped mountains rolled
onwards into infinity. Massive, brooding.

Ashley shivered and drew her tweed coat closer
around her. She was awed by the magnificence of these
ancient peaks, and she longed to explore the landscape
and discover this aloof country that had bred Lucas and
bequeathed him its own fierce dignity.

The road curved and dropped towards the village of
Tremblant and the hotel the company would be using
during their stay in Quebec.

Ashley's heart started to beat painfully. The thought
of seeing Lucas again was almost unbearable. But not as
unbearable as the possibility of not seeing him.

Tim drove into the forecourt of the hotel. 'Here we
are, beautiful! Home! At least for a couple of weeks.'

Before he had a chance to leap out and open the door
for her a tall lanky figure bundled up in a sheepskin coat
came swiftly out of the hotel and wrenched her door
open. It was Lucas, and he was scowling.

'You were supposed to be travelling in the make-up
winnebago,' he said accusingly.

'Tim very kindly offered to drive me instead.' Ashley
forced herself to sound composed, although that was the
last thing she was feeling.

Tim leaned across her to speak to his stern-faced boss. 'I needed company, Luc,' he said, 'and beautiful here managed to make the trip seem short.' He looked surprised. 'It didn't matter, did it? We're not late, are we?'

'No, it didn't matter,' Lucas owned grudgingly. 'I just wish people wouldn't change things when they've been set up, that's all. But you're here now, let's forget it!' He helped Ashley—none too gently—to climb out of the car. 'I'll take care of her now, Tim,' he said shortly. 'You'd better park on the back lot. They don't want a lot of extra vehicles cluttering the main entrance. Then Maggy wants to see you. She's in chalet 74.' He dismissed the perplexed boy curtly and started pulling Ashley towards the hotel. She shook off his hand and stopped dead in the snow-covered path.

'I'm perfectly capable of signing the register unaided!' she snapped. She was brittle with outrage.

'What's the matter with you *now*?' he grated angrily.

'I don't enjoy being treated like a . . . like a piece of luggage!' she hissed. 'You haul me around as if I was a parcel!'

'And *I* don't enjoy waiting for the winnebago only to find you've decided to go gallivanting off with Tim Webber,' he loomed over her like an avenging angel.

'I'd hardly call it gallivanting,' she countered. 'What's it got to do with you anyway?' She was elated that her plan to annoy him seemed to have succeeded.

He answered her savagely. 'You listen to me, Ashley Morrison! I don't give a damn what you do with your private life in your *own time*. But you're here to work—not go for romantic drives with my assistants.'

'I wasn't aware that highway 401 was particularly romantic,' she retorted. 'Did it seem that way to you and Miss Sheppard?'

They faced each other, their breath white mist in the cold air.

'I left early in order to meet the caravan when it

arrived,' he said. 'I wanted to show you Tremblant before it got dark.'

'Not being psychic I didn't know you'd made these plans.' She looked at him with disdain, but her haughtiness was ruined by an immense shiver that ran from the soles of her feet to the crown of her rufous head. She felt as if a tub of ice water had been emptied over her. The sun was sinking and the cold was becoming intense, and while the tweed culottes Aunt Constance had remodelled out of an old skirt were smart, they weren't particularly warm.

'Oh, lord! You're not getting pneumonia now, are you?' Lucas started hurrying her towards the hotel entrance. 'Get in the warm. The last thing I need is an actress with the sniffles.'

Typical! thought Ashley resentfully; all he cares about is his beastly film, once it's finished I could drop dead at his feet and he wouldn't even notice.

The warm lobby was a relief after the chill. She signed the register and collected her chalet key. As they were leaving Lucas said:

'Before you do anything else I advise you to change into your long-johns.'

She stared at him. 'Into my *what*?'

'Long woollen underwear. You're certainly going to need it tomorrow on the shoot.' He looked at her suspiciously. 'You do *have* long underwear, I hope?'

'I'm afraid I don't . . . no one mentioned . . .'

'No problem,' he said easily, 'I've got a jeep. I'll drive you into the village and you can buy some at one of the ski boutiques.'

He started for the door, but she hung back.

'I can't buy anything, Lucas,' she explained, 'not right now.'

'Why not? The stores stay open late around the slopes.'

'It's not that. I don't have any spare cash.' Her heart-shaped face was now suffused with pink, for she was in an agony of embarrassment.

His eyes narrowed. 'Didn't Maggy give you your per diems?'

'Yes, but it's . . . it's gone . . . that is . . .' Before she could decide whether to explain the situation to him or not he had turned on her in fury.

'Ashley, you're *impossible!*' He spoke through gritted teeth. 'I suppose you blew the lot on that little silver number you were wearing last night.' He struck his forehead. 'I knew I shouldn't have let you loose in Yorkville. You're the most extravagant . . .' He made an effort and calmed down slightly. 'I will lend you the money to buy some suitable underwear,' he said. 'Come on, before the stores close.'

It was too late now telling him that she'd sent her money home to England. He'd just think she was making excuses. Still she hung back.

'Please, Lucas, I don't need any . . . long underwear . . .' In spite of herself she giggled—it did seem the most peculiar subject to be arguing about! He continued urging her towards his jeep that was parked nearby.

'Get your priorities straight,' he snapped. 'If you catch a chill your work will suffer. You owe it to me to stay healthy.'

There was no point discussing it with him, so she kept quiet and climbed into the jeep.

They drove on the white snowy roads into a fairy-tale village which twinkled with lights in the early dusk, and parked in front of a shop with a window display featuring skis and ski equipment.

'Lucas, this is a temporary loan only,' she insisted before they went in. 'I intend to pay you back.'

'You bet your boots you'll pay me back,' he said curtly. 'I'm not in the habit of buying women their underwear.'

'And I'm not in the habit of having it bought for me!' Ashley flashed back.

He looked at her laconically. 'I should hope not indeed,' he said, giving her a gentle push into the boutique.

She chose long thermal ski-underwear patterned with snowflakes, and a long-sleeved vest to match since he insisted she would need it.

'Do you own a parka?' he asked. 'Or is this all you've got?' He fingered her tweed coat disparagingly.

'I don't know what a parka *is*.'

'The closest thing would be an anorak, I guess. Except a parka's down-filled and a hundred per cent warmer. You'll need one for the Quebec climate.' He turned to the salesgirl. 'Maybe we should look at some snow-suits while we're here,' he said.

When the girl had left Ashley turned to him in concern. 'I don't want to spend too much, Lucas,' she said. 'Remember I still have to send money back to England for . . . for . . .'

'Ah yes! Your national debt. Your reason for slumming with the film,' he remarked nastily. 'Don't be dumb, Ashley. Warm clothing's necessary for the job. I'll have the office deduct a bit from your salary cheque each week. That way it won't hurt as much. And let this be a lesson to you,' he went on loftily. 'Remember silver jump-suits may be cute, but they don't keep you warm at thirty below zero.'

The salesgirl arrived with several down-filled snow-suits—eiderdown-like garments, zippered up the sides of the legs and high at the neck. Ashley was so slim that she succeeded in looking quite trim in spite of all the padding. They were light and very warm, made of nylon fabric and they came in a variety of colours.

'The slate-blue looks lovely on you, madam,' the salesgirl assured her, and turned to Lucas. 'Don't you agree, sir? That the blue sets off your wife's colouring best.'

Ashley turned beet-red, but Lucas merely smiled. 'I like her in blue,' he agreed. 'Which one do *you* prefer, honey?' he asked Ashley pleasantly, his eyes glinting with mischief.

'The *cheapest*.' He could not know how deeply this game hurt her, but she hated him for his flippancy.

'Nonsense, honey! My wife's inclined to scrimp on

herself,' he explained. 'We'll take the blue, and hang the expense.' He put a husbandly arm round Ashley's rigid shoulders. She suffered this embrace until the salesgirl bustled away to pack up the suit.

Before they left he also bought her a woollen toque. 'So your ears don't freeze off between shots,' he said—and armed with boxes, they finally drove away.

In the jeep he noticed her set face. 'Lord, you're like a broody hen, Ashley! What's got into you now? That charade at the store?'

'Something like that,' she said quietly. Little did he know her real feelings.

'Well, don't worry about it,' his eyes were hooded, 'I should think we've as much chance of winding up at the altar as a snowball in hell.'

'Yes.' This caused the cheerless little cloud on Ashley's mental horizon to grow darker.

She noticed the jeep was climbing away from the direction of the hotel. 'Isn't the hotel back that way?' She pointed behind them.

'That's right.'

'Where are we going, then?'

'I have to deliver some script changes to Sloane,' he said, 'we're driving to her cottage. She stipulated she get one to herself, rather than stay at the hotel with the rest of us.' His jaw was set.

'You could have dropped me off first.' She shrank from seeing Sloane and Lucas together.

'The script changes concern you too. Besides, I want you to get to know Sloane better.'

Why does he want that?' Ashley wondered. Does he guess I'm beginning to care for him, and wants to make quite sure I understand that he's already committed to Sloane? But this didn't fit in with his image of philanderer. It was much more likely to be an ego trip for him to be with two women, both of whom desired him. Well, she wouldn't show him, not by the flicker of an eyelash, that she found him attractive. His ego could go begging!

They drew up outside a fair-sized A-frame house set in

the side of the mountain. It was dark now and huge crystal stars swung in the dark night sky vying with the cluster of lights in the village below.

Lucas came around to her side of the jeep. Before she had time to think he put his strong hands around her waist and lifted her out. Automatically her hands rested on his broad shoulders as he swung her into the cold night air. He did not immediately put her down, but held her close. His sheepskin coat was open and she could feel his warmth pressed against her. Her petal-soft cheek lay against his, and she heard his breath catch. For a few blissful seconds she let herself be held in this silent embrace, then she pushed her body away from his and struggled to be put down. She could see his eyes, like black pools in the shadows, searching her face.

'Ashley,' he said hoarsely.

Using all the will-power she could command, she forced herself to say lightly:

'Brrr, it's cold! Do you think it's going to snow?' Not the brightest remark, in view of the cloudless sky.

The planes of his face grew harsher, and wordlessly he turned from her and led the way to the door of the smart house, rapping on it with unwarranted ferocity.

A middle-aged woman—Sloane's dresser—let them in and showed them into the firelit living area. The polished floor gleamed in the dancing light of a log fire. Handwoven rugs lay about, and the room smelt pleasantly of burning apple boughs, and a muskier, sophisticated scent which was Sloane's perfume, made for her exclusively in Paris. Ashley soon learnt that wherever the movie star was, a subtle cloud of this distinctive perfume surrounded her like an aura.

'Luc darling!' Sloane stood at the entrance of the room, casually immaculate. Her long coltish legs accentuated by tight violet-shaded raw-silk slacks. A diaphanous black blouse was artfully knotted at her waist and her feet were bare. She caught sight of Ashley and her radiant smile faded. 'Oh! hello—Ashby, isn't it?'

'Ash*ley*. Good evening, Miss Sheppard. I hope I'm not intruding,' said Ashley, although it was clear she

was. She was very aware that her culottes were creased
from the journey, and her hair, which she had left
unshampooed at Lucas's command, was beginning to
lose its usual glossy sheen. Sloane took this in too, and
her expression changed from irritation to contempt. She
indicated chairs before the fire, and when they were
seated she curled up on the rug near Lucas's feet. He
remained impassive, staring abstractedly into the
flames.

'Ash*ley*. Of course! The girl in silver. You must call
me Sloane. After all, if we're going to be working
together we mustn't be formal.' Her deep red mouth
curved in a smile, but in spite of her apparent friendli-
ness Ashley didn't feel at ease. There was an air of
hypocrisy about Sloane Sheppard. She seemed always to
be putting on an act. Now she twisted round and tapped
Lucas's knee familiarly.

'What's all this about changes in the script, darling?'

He stood up to get his coat, lifting Sloane's hand off
his leg as if it were an old glove. He pulled some papers
out of an inner pocket.

'Here,' he said, 'not much, but it concerns tomorrow's
set-up. The scene with Ashley. I wanted you both to get
a look, and read the scene for me now.' He handed both
women the altered pages, then went to sit on an upright
chair away from the fire. The shadows exaggerated the
hollows in his face, making it appear harsher.

She got up from the floor and switched on two table
lamps. 'What a bore you are, darling,' she said mildly
enough. 'As if it isn't enough making us leave Toronto at
the crack this morning, because you *have* to get here
before the others. Now you want me to work! I thought
we might go out for dinner.' She smiled conspiratorially
at Ashley. 'Isn't he a brute?' she pouted. 'What *shall* I do
with him?'

Ashley smiled weakly. She found Sloane's archness
disagreeable. The woman seemed to be the embodiment
of everything that was false in the world of the theatre.

'Let's get on with it, shall we, Sloane?' said Lucas,
sounding weary. 'We haven't got all night.'

Eyes narrowed, Sloane said, 'Do you want action or just a straight reading?'

'Just read it. I want to hear how it sounds.' He shadowed his eyes with his hand.

Ashley was suddenly a victim of terrible stage-fright. Although the scene was only a few lines she was conscious that she was going to be reading with a very experienced film star, and was being assessed by Lucas, who was, according to all reports, a first rate director. But her stage discipline asserted itself, and she controlled the butterflies madly whirling around in her tummy and concentrated on the script.

In the re-written scene Ashley's character—Elizabeth—is told of her father's accidental death. It was a very intense moment in the film, and a difficult one to play.

They read it through several times, and soon Ashley forgot her nervousness and really got into the feeling of the scene. She was surprised that Sloane read so quietly that sometimes she had difficulty hearing her.

After a while Lucas stopped them. 'That'll do for now,' he said, 'we'll work on it tomorrow morning. It's coming. But, Ashley, tone it down a bit . . . it's too big.'

'But isn't she feeling very emotional? I mean to say, her father's just been killed.' Her rounded chin tilted obstinately.

'We'll discuss it tomorrow morning,' he said, dismissing her. Then he picked up their coats from a chair by the door. 'Have you had dinner yet, Sloane?'

The sultry star stretched like a sleek black cat. 'I thought you'd never ask, darling,' she purred. She indicated her bare feet. 'Just give me time to put on some boots and I'm ready. Or do you want to go somewhere dressy?'

They both ignored Ashley, who stood between them feeling very much in the way and burning with resentment.

'No need to change, Sloane,' said Lucas. 'We've an early start tomorrow, so let's eat at the hotel. The *three* of us.' He looked directly at Ashley for the first time since they had come into the room.

'Thank you very much,' she said, jerking her coat away from him, 'but I have a date for dinner . . . at least I think I have,' she added, remembering Tim's tentative offer.

'What do you mean, you *think* you have?' Lucas snapped.

'Well, I'm not sure, but Tim did suggest . . .' she faltered.

'Oh, Tim! He'll be too busy to take you anywhere,' Lucas said bossily. 'No, we'll eat at the hotel, along with Maggy and the rest of the gang.' He threw Sloane a warning glance. 'Like a proper company.'

'Luc's very big on company solidarity,' the brunette spoke confidentially to Ashley, 'so I guess we must humour the brute. You'll have to have your date some other time. I think it's too *sweet*,' she continued condescendingly, 'about you and Tim.'

Ashley was about to deny any romantic involvement with Tim, but stopped herself. If Lucas thought she had fallen for Tim he would never guess about her growing attraction to him. Better remain silent. Besides, this misunderstanding kept Sloane civil, for if she thought Ashley was interested in someone, it meant she was no threat. Although with her wrinkled clothes and dirty hair Ashley failed to see how she could be regarded as a threat by anyone.

Out in the hall Sloane pulled on a pair of high-heeled suede boots and snuggled herself into a luxurious dark mink coat. 'What car are you driving, Luc?' she asked. When he told her the jeep she shuddered with exaggerated horror. 'No *way*, darling!' she exclaimed. 'We'll take my car. You can collect your tin can later on tonight.' She looked quite pleased with herself, but Lucas overrode these plans.

'You can take your car if you like, but I'm taking the jeep. I have to work with Maggy after dinner, and I want to get a reasonably early night.'

'Then Ashley will go with me,' said Sloane, 'if you're

going to be so difficult.' She imperiously beckoned Ashley and led the way to her Oldsmobile. Trailing behind Sloane's glamorous mink-clad form, Ashley felt even more creased and travel-stained than ever.

'Thank God my agent insists on a rented car as part of my contract,' said Sloane, 'otherwise Luc would have me crawling in and out of those poisonous jeeps for the entire shoot.' She slid behind the wheel and checked her face in the rear-view mirror before starting the motor. 'He's *divine*,' she went on, as they drove away, 'and of course I adore him. But sometimes I don't think he's always very *perceptive*,' she glanced briefly at Ashley, her face a beautiful oval blank. 'That business about your reading of the scene we just did, for example. The one he said was too big. Well, I must say I thought your reading was just right. Between us girls, Ashley, I sometimes think Luc tends to shy away from *real* emotion in his films. Take my advice, darling, play it the way you read it. Don't be *too* swayed by Luc.' She smiled again, her eyes opaque with innocence.

Ashley couldn't help feeling pleased, even if she did dislike the woman. It's always nice to be praised. And to be praised by a professional of Sloane's standing was particularly welcome. Only Sloane's dismissal of Lucas's abilities seemed strange. It was contrary to everything Ashley had been told by others who had worked for him. She didn't have time to pursue the point, however, for by that time they had arrived back at the hotel.

Lucas was waiting for them in the lobby.

'I've sent Tim in to keep four seats at the company table,' he said. He was looking irritated, and cast a distinctly baleful look in Ashley's direction.

The long company table was nearly full when they arrived. Tim waved at Ashley and indicated to a seat next to him.

'I've reserved two seats for you and Sloane at the other end, Luc,' he said.

'Couldn't you get four together?' Lucas growled. 'Oh, forget it,' he said, when Tim started to explain. 'But I want to see you about this week's expense accounts right after dinner, Tim. Understood?'

'Sure, Luc,' agreed Tim, looking rather puzzled, 'anything you say.'

Lucas strode off to sit at the far end of the table, where Sloane was already holding court.

'What's up with him?' Tim nodded at Lucas's retreating back. 'Did he and La Sheppard have a row?'

'I think he's just being his usual grumpy self,' Ashley observed.

'Oh, Luc's not grumpy,' said Tim, 'not unless something's upsetting him. I would have thought he'd have been all sweetness and light now he's reunited with his old flame.'

'Reunited, yes,' said Ashley, crumbling a wholewheat roll and feeling perceptibly depressed by this conversation.

'Never mind about them,' Tim dismissed them, 'I'm sorry about our dinner date, beautiful. I was all set to take you to L'Esterel, but when I told Luc he got all huffy and suddenly dug up all this work. We'll have to take a rain-check. OK?'

'It's probably just as well, Tim,' said Ashley, feeling a little heartened by this last bit of information. 'I do have an early start tomorrow, and this is a working trip, after all. I can't risk making Lucas grumpier by being half asleep on the job.'

Tim looked discouraged. 'OK. But you must agree to let me take you out somewhere nice for dinner before we go back to Toronto, Ashley.'

'Let's see, Tim, shall we?' She tried to be diplomatic. 'Right now all I really have time for is my role in this film. Let's just play it by ear. Will you settle for that?'

'Do I have a choice?'

'Not really, no,' she smiled apologetically.

'OK, beautiful!' he said. 'But don't be surprised if I keep pestering you.'

She smiled, then deliberately changed the subject, getting him to describe his side of the movie business.

She enjoyed her dinner, particularly when she discovered she could charge it to her bill and pay for it out of her next per diem money, and she relished the ham steak garnished with pineapple and cherries, accompanied by candied sweet potatoes, that were drenched in dark brown sugar and melted in her mouth.

She had just swallowed her last mouthful of lemon sherbet, which had followed the main dish, when Lucas materialised behind her chair. He spoke to Tim.

'We're meeting in Maggy's chalet in ten minutes,' he said, 'and we'll need that list of figures.'

Tim hastily drained his coffee cup. 'Right, Luc, I'll go and fetch them now.' He got up and turned to Ashley. ''Night, beautiful! See you at the crack of dawn. Sleep well.'

After he had gone Lucas took his chair at her side. Ashley stirred sugar into her coffee.

'Don't you have to get to that meeting too, Lucas?' She asked, not looking at him.

'Not for ten minutes,' he said. 'I came to take you back to your chalet.'

She looked at him now, her green-flecked eyes enormous. 'But it's only a few yards down the hill. I don't need an escort.'

'What a gracious female you are,' he said acidly. 'Anyway, all your parcels are in my jeep. I'll carry them for you.'

'They're really not heavy, Lucas,' she resisted him, not wanting a repetition of last night's humiliation.

'Oh, drink your coffee and shut up!' he snarled, 'I haven't got all night.'

Wordlessly she pushed aside her full cup and went for her coat, refusing his help when he tried to assist her. They went out into the night silently, each of them grim-lipped, Ashley pink and Lucas pale with suppressed anger. Silently Lucas collected her parcels, and together they turned and walked down the hill, a foot apart, and simmering. The tight-packed snow crunched under their feet.

They reached the chalet and, stony-faced, she held

out her hands for her packages. He glowered at her and
dropped them at her feet, where they skidded on the icy
path.

'Thank you *very* much.' Her voice was clipped with
rage.

Lucas made a sound that could have been an oath or a
groan, and grabbing her in his arms he crushed his
mouth on hers. His teeth grazed her closed lips, and
his arms held her so tightly she thought her ribs might
crack.

She was so surprised by this onslaught that at first she
did not fight him but stayed unmoving in his cruel
embrace. Then she desperately tried to turn her head
away from his punishing mouth, to free her arms that he
had pinioned to her sides.

As suddenly as he had swooped down on her he let her
go, and they faced each other in the moonlight. They
were both pale now—pale and shaking.

'That's so you won't feel deprived,' he rasped. 'Tim
would have been sure to have kissed you goodnight if
he'd brought you back here.'

She stared at him. Her lips felt bruised and swollen
after his brutal kiss.

Without another word he turned and walked away,
his broad shoulders hunched, his hands buried in the
pockets of his sheepskin coat.

Trembling, Ashley collected her parcels and went into
her room. Even after she had washed her face and
prepared for bed she could still feel the imprint of his
violent lips on hers.

She set her alarm clock and turned out the light, but
she could not erase the memory of the last half hour, and
lay unrelaxed under the covers trying to fathom out what
she had done to provoke him.

Wasn't it enough that the beautiful Sloane Sheppard
was crazy about him? Did he want every female within
sight to fawn over him the way Sloane did?

I'd rather die first! Ashley thought, trying to get
comfortable in the wide hotel bed.

But she had wanted his kiss. Since last night she had

dreamed of practically nothing else. But when it had finally occurred, the angry embrace he had bestowed on her had turned her gentle dream into a nightmare.

CHAPTER SIX

It seemed to Ashley that she had just fallen into a deep well of sleep when she was dragged to the surface by the shrill sound of bells. She lay still for a moment, not knowing where she was. Then she realised that the noise was her alarm clock. Five-thirty a.m.! Time to get up. She staggered into the bathroom and blearily looked in the mirror, she found it hard to focus her sleep-drugged eyes at this hour of the morning.

Like an automaton she showered and dressed in her new quilted snow-suit, and was just pulling the woollen toque down over her ears when there was a soft tap at the door. The car was ready to drive her to the location.

It was still pitch dark outside and freezing. The shock of the cold blanched her face. She sat next to the driver, but they didn't talk, it was too early for conversation. Ashley contented herself by peering sleepily at the vague silhouettes of tree-topped mountains which grew more distinct as the night faded.

They drove north, then took a turning and cautiously went along a narrow road which led to massive Mont Tremblant Park. They crossed a log bridge over Devil's River, so named because of its treacherous rapids, and climbed towards the Rangers' Lodge, which the film company had commandeered for the duration of the shoot.

Ashley stumbled out of the car into a dawn-tinted world with sky the colour of opals. The snow was so bright it hurt her sleep-heavy eyes. Beyond the circle of open ground in front of the Lodge the dense forest stretched, dark and full of deep silence. Only the sound of the wind whistled in the trees. But in the area of the Lodge there was bustle, even at this ungodly hour, and when she entered the low-ceilinged building she was greeted by a blast of warm air, bright lights, and the tantalising smell of fresh-brewed coffee.

'Hi, Ashley!' Jane greeted her. 'Have some breakfast before we start on your make-up.'

Jane was standing before a trestle table which held an enormous coffee urn and enough food to feed an army. There were rolls and croissants, bagels and sliced black bread, there were slabs of sweet butter and cream cheese, jams, marmalades and fresh fruit, Danish pastries and doughnuts and coffee-rings; two huge jugs of orange juice, several cartons of cream, and a sack of sugar.

Ashley learned, while making *Time of Trial*, that it is customary for the company to provide meals on the spot during filming for all involved, but she was so dazed that first morning she thought for a moment that she had stumbled by accident into some early morning party.

Gratefully she took the styrofoam cup of coffee offered, then ate a Danish pastry and some fruit. After this hasty meal she went to a curtained-off section of the rustic building which served as the wardrobe room. There she put on her costume over her new long warm underwear and made her way to the make-up winnebago where Jane carefully hollowed her cheeks and added dark smudges under her eyes for the scene. Then the first A.D. came to fetch her.

The scene was being shot in a small hut that was intended for storing snow removal equipment. The designer had fixed it to resemble a log cabin of the period. The actual acting area was tiny, and the rest of the hut was filled with arc-lamps, coils of wire and cable, wooden boxes, and parka-clad figures moving to and fro in the shadows behind the brilliant lights.

Lucas was in a huddle with his cameraman. He was also wearing a bulky parka, but his wild black head was bare, and in spite of the casualness of his outfit he exuded an aura of authority.

Ashley's heart did a somersault when she caught sight of him, but she made herself sit on an apple box, as they were called, and study her script calmly in spite of its insistent hammering.

Sloane came into the hut huddled up in her mink. She had her own winnebago where she was made-up and had her hair done. She looked magnificent, her long raven hair braided with beads into two thick plaits, an Indian headband round her smooth forehead. Her costume, under the mink, was made of buckskin, elaborately embroidered and fringed. She looked clean and shining, and Ashley, examining her fingernails, cut short and blackened for authenticity, felt grubby and plain. Claire had tied her glorious red hair back with a strip of dirty linen, and several strands had been pulled loose to cling limply to her dirt-streaked face. Her costume looked filthy, and brown greasepaint had been rubbed into her neck. She felt a mess, and when Lucas came towards her she felt at a distinct disadvantage beside the beautiful Sloane Sheppard.

He greeted the two women courteously. His manner was totally neutral. If it had not been for the fact that her lips still bore traces of his bruising kisses Ashley might have thought she had imagined the whole episode last night.

'Let's have a look at you, Ashley,' he said, staring fixedly into her dirty face. Then, nodding with satisfaction, he took her hands and examined them.

She was like an animal hypnotised into submission. Her hands lay in his warm ones, and wave after wave of sensation flowed through her. She felt weak with pleasure at his touch.

It must be the early morning, she thought, either that or I'm going mad. But whatever the explanation she had not the will to draw her hands away—and he did not release them.

'Luc, if we're going to hang about here I shall go back to my winnebago!' Sloane sounded petulant, and her carefully made-up brows were creased with annoyance.

Reluctantly Lucas let go of Ashley's hands. 'Just checking the make-up, Sloane,' he said equably. 'Let's have a look at you now.' After a moment he called for

Jane, who sped to his side, her many-pocketed make-up apron filled with powder-jars and pencils.

'What happened, Jane?' he asked. 'I thought we agreed on the hand make-up back in Toronto. Why isn't Sloane wearing it?'

Jane looked uncomfortable. 'Well, Sloane . . . that is . . .'

'I'm not having that muck on *my* hands, Luc!' Sloane said loudly. 'She can wear it if she likes,' she pointed rudely at Ashley, 'but not me!'

'Now, sweetie, let's be professional about this.' To Ashley's astonishment Lucas didn't lose his temper. He spoke soothingly to his star, treating her like a wayward child rather than a full-grown woman. 'You're playing the part of an Indian woman, sweetie. And while you don't have to look a mess like Ashley does—' Thanks a lot! thought Ashley—'nevertheless you would *not* have nails that looked as if they'd just been manicured by Elizabeth Arden. So I want you to let Jane cut them, and put some make-up on your beautiful hands and then for God's sake let's get *started!*' The honey in his voice was starting to turn to vinegar. He took a deep breath and put his arm round Sloane's shoulders. 'OK, Sloane? Will you do that for me?'

She fluttered her lashes and her full red mouth pouted. '*Brute!*' she said in a nauseating 'baby' voice. 'All right—dirty puddies, then, if you insist.' She turned up her face to be kissed and after a moment's hesitation Lucas hastily pecked her cheek.

A searing flame of jealousy shot through Ashley. She felt sick at the display she had just witnessed. How could he tolerate such behaviour? She had expected him to wipe the floor with Sloane, not toady to her in such a disgusting fashion. Maggy caught her eye and gave her a knowing look while making a dumb show of strangling Sloane behind her back.

But Ashley didn't smile. She was still too shaken by the awful jealousy that had swept over her when she had seen Lucas put his arm round Sloane and kiss her cheek. She had never felt such an emotion in her life before, had never realised how aptly the Shakespearean name for jealousy—'the green sickness'—described it. She did indeed feel green and ill at the very thought of Lucas kissing Sloane, or anybody else for that matter. And she was a mass of contradictions when she thought of him—filled one moment with longing for him, the next moment hating him for causing her to feel this way.

Eventually they started on the scene, a two-shot with very little movement. Lucas rehearsed them a few times, then there was a scurry of activity while wardrobe assistants hovered around, and Jane and Claire fussed over hair and make-up.

'OK,' said Lucas, 'let's try for a take. Now remember, Ashley, wait for me to say 'action' and don't stop till I say "cut".'

'All right,' she replied, her heart thumping with stage fright.

Lucas checked with his cameraman. The sound man started his tape rolling. A voice called—'Speed—mark it!' and Ashley nearly jumped out of her skin when a boy slapped the clapperboard a few inches from her face and read the slate.

'Scene 76. Take one!' he bellowed.

'*Action!*' Lucas said crisply, and Ashley and Sloane started their scene.

They repeated it many times, take after take. To quell her nerves Ashley surreptitiously did breathing exercises between takes and her voice grew stronger. After a while the sound man came over to her.

'Could you cut down on your volume a wee bit, lassie?' he said. 'You nearly blew my head off that last take.'

'Sorry,' Ashley grew pink, 'I'm so used to projecting my voice.'

'Yes, do tone it down, for God's sake, Ashley,' said Lucas. 'Stop trying to show us all how to act, and *think* about the role instead.'

Ashley bit her lip. The injustice of Lucas's attitude to her rankled. He'd kissed and cajoled Sloane when she'd behaved like a spoilt child, but he was barely civil to her when she was trying her best. She *hated* him! She would take Sloane's advice and play the scene the way she felt like doing it, and ignore his direction.

After many more takes Lucas called a halt. 'Now we'll take the close-ups,' he said. 'Take a break, girls, while we change the lighting.'

Sloane went to her winnebago, and Ashley, wrapped in the jacket of her snow-suit, sat huddled on a rickety folding chair watching the head grip adjust the flags on the lights. It took a long time. She was learning that one of the first things necessary in film acting is immense patience.

Maggy came over to her, her stop-watch dangling on a cord round her neck, her hands in woollen mittens so she could write without being totally frozen. She handed Ashley a cup of coffee.

'Here, honey! You look as if you could use this.'

Gratefully Ashley sipped the hot drink. Her teeth were chattering in spite of her parka, for it was chill once she had left the brilliantly lit area of the set.

'Take it easy, Ashley,' said Maggy. 'Don't try so hard, honey.'

'I *have* to try hard,' Ashley answered miserably. 'If I don't try hard I'll never get it.'

'Of course you have to try,' Maggy agreed,' but don't *push* it so. Listen to Luc.'

'*Him!*' Ashley's voice wobbled with emotion, for the truth was she was very close to tears. It had been a tense morning and she could tell that the scene wasn't working, and it wasn't working because of her, and she didn't know what to do about it. She was starting to panic.

'Yeah—*him!*' Maggy grinned.

Ashley refused to smile back. 'I don't understand him, Maggy,' she confided. 'How *could* he toady to Sloane like that this morning! It was disgusting!'

'Oh, that!' Maggy dismissed the episode airily. 'If he'd been tough with La Sheppard the way she'd deserved she'd probably have flounced off the set and the entire morning would have been shot. He was being diplomatic. He knows his stuff, Ashley—really. Trust him.'

She bustled away to check the amount of film needed for the rest of the morning.

Trust him? How could she do that? Ashley reflected bitterly. His behaviour the past two days hadn't exactly built up her confidence! When he wasn't tantalising her, he was leaping on her and kissing her with such ferocity that he frightened her. And what frightened her even more was that in spite of this irrational conduct she knew she was falling deeper and deeper in love with him. Even while she was hating him for unwittingly putting her through these emotional hoops.

The lights were finally ready and she took her position in front of the camera. Jane powdered her face while Claire fiddled with her hair.

'That last scene was an establishing long shot, Ashley,' Lucas explained. 'A two-shot of you and Sloane. Now we're coming in for a close-up of you for the same scene, so do exactly what you did before. Remember it's the same scene, but this time I'm shooting it from Sloane's P.O.V.'

She looked at him through hostile eyes. 'What's a "P.O.V."?'

'Point of View—a technical term. Did you understand the rest of what I told you?'

She nodded dumbly. She noticed that Lucas looked drawn and worried. Come to that, she felt drawn and worried herself. She couldn't seem to get into the scene no matter how hard she tried. She missed having an audience to play to, and she found it very difficult having to remain static rather than use big gestures.

'Are we ready?' said Lucas. 'Where's Sloane?'

'She's still in her winnebago, Luc.' Maggy was clearly put out. 'She said you wouldn't need her for Ashley's close-ups.'

Lucas's lips went thin with annoyance. 'Will someone tell Miss Sheppard I expect her on the set *immediately*. Tell her I give her one minute, after that I'll have her *carried* here.' His voice was quiet, but the menace in it made Ashley's hair stand on end. He began pacing, like a dangerous caged animal. No one moved or spoke on the set. You could have heard a feather, let alone a pin, drop.

It seemed like an eternity, although actually it was only minutes, when the door opened and Sloane came in.

'Luc, *really*! You don't need me for this shot, surely? I'm not even on-camera.' Her tortoiseshell eyes were hard as pebbles.

'That's what I've always liked about you, Sloane,' Lucas said with deceptive amiability, 'your generosity to other actors. Don't you think it might be difficult for Ashley if you're not here to give her her cues?'

'*Everything* seems difficult for her,' Sloane said unkindly. 'Let's face it, darling—you're probably not going to be able to use any of today's footage, so why waste my time? Get one of the grips to read her cues.'

Ashley felt the blood drain from her body. She wanted to die with humiliation. It was bad enough knowing she wasn't doing a good job without having Sloane broadcast it to all and sundry.

Lucas's hand shot out and he grabbed the older woman tightly round her wrist. 'It's difficult for anybody their first day on a film set,' he rasped. 'I seem to remember that you weren't exactly brilliant yourself when you started. You will now stand beside the camera and feed Ashley her cues, and try to *help* her . . . help all of us . . . as much as you can.' He released Sloane's arm.

Everybody on the set held their breath. The dark-haired beauty thoughtfully rubbed her wrist before speaking. 'Well, if you're going to *bully* me, darling, I don't have a choice, do I?' She had apparently decided not to fight back. 'It just seemed rather a waste of time, that's all. Under the *circumstances*.' She tilted her head slightly in Ashley's direction, leaving no doubt in anyone's mind as to her low opinion of Ashley's talent.

The morning dragged on at a snail's pace for Ashley. There seemed to be so much to remember. If Lucas

wasn't yelling 'cut' in the middle of the scene because she
was playing it too 'theatrically', then it was Maggy telling
her, 'You had your hand at your throat on that line
Ashley,' or, 'You leaned on the table at that point
before.'

Not only had she to remember her lines and infuse
them with the same emotion again and again, but she
also had to constantly remember her exact movements
and gestures which had to be duplicated for each take.

And she had thought film acting was easy! Today's
experience had proved it to be anything but. Already she
had respect for all actors in that medium, and a growing
doubt that she would ever be able to master it. She
understood now why Lucas had been so angry when
she had originally refused his offer with such contempt.
He had wanted to teach her a lesson, and in one
short, humiliating morning he had more than proved his
point.

The afternoon was spent doing 'reverse shots'. This
time it was Ashley's turn to stand by the camera and give
cues to Sloane. She watched Sloane carefully. The star's
face looked almost expressionless, her eyes steady and
unblinking, her delivery so casual and her voice so soft
that again Ashley had trouble hearing her. Everything
she did—in front of the camera—was understated and
low key.

Ashley began to think the A.D. would never call out,
'It's a wrap!' but eventually he did, and the day's work
was over. Numbly she removed her costume, wiped off
her make-up, and dressed in her own clothes again.

As she was leaving Maggy called to her and suggested
that they drive back to the hotel together. Ashley agreed
readily and the two women left the park together.

The sun was setting behind the mountains and the
snow and sky were stained a mauvish-pink. Clouds like
tattered silk changed their shape in the strong north
wind that was starting to blow. In spite of her depression
Ashley forgot her troubles long enough to admire the
magnificent sunset.

'Oh, Maggy—look,' she said, 'that sky! It's the colour

of . . . of amethysts.' She pressed close to the car window.

'That's a Quebec sky. Usually means we'll get snow before long. Good—we need snow for tomorrow,' was Maggy's practical answer. Ashley was beginning to realise that film people always seemed to connect everything with their work. She leaned back in her seat and stifled a weary yawn.

Maggy looked at her sympathetically. 'Tired, eh?'

'Tired? I'm *dead*!' Ashley admitted. 'Five-thirty seems eons ago. I feel as if I've been up for forty-eight hours!'

'Then you'll be happy to hear we're not shooting until later in the morning tomorrow,' said Maggy.

A foreboding that something was wrong filled Ashley. 'Why not?' she asked.

'Lucas is getting today's footage processed in Montreal tonight. He wants to get a look at it in the morning before deciding what to shoot next.'

'Because of me?' queried Ashley in a small voice. 'Because of my work today?' She was beginning to feel paranoid.

Maggy looked at Ashley's white face compassionately. 'I honestly don't know, honey,' she said, 'but may I give you a bit of advice? Strictly off the record.'

Ashley nodded, a chill of apprehension spreading over her.

'Don't fight Luc all the time. On the set today I had the feeling that you were deliberately not paying attention to him. Don't you like him?'

'I . . . I'm not sure.' She gulped back the truth. 'We didn't hit it off too well at first in London.'

'Well, take it from me, honey, Luc is a *prince*.' Maggy's foot pressed down on the accelerator in her enthusiasm and the car skidded slightly on the icy road. 'I don't usually tell people this,' she continued when she'd regained control of the car, 'because Luc wouldn't like it, but when Dan died I went completely to pieces. Had a breakdown and couldn't work for quite a while . . . and there was no money. Luc paid for everything.

Dan's funeral, the rent . . . you name it. He's like a
father to little Bobby. He's great with kids, and Bobby
adores him. He got me my first job when I recovered,
and absolutely refused to let me pay him back. He's the
kindest man living, Ashley, and a great director.
I'm only telling you this because it might help you to
know the sort of man you're working for. Might help
you get rid of that prejudice you seem to be carrying
around.'

Ashley's mouth tiptilted into a lopsided grin. 'Thanks,
Maggy,' she said, 'I appreciate you trying to help me. I
just hope it's not too late.'

There was no one around the hotel when they returned. Tim had driven to Montreal to get the film
processed. The other actors had gone to another village
for dinner, and Lucas was nowhere to be seen. Ashley
was so exhausted she barely had the strength to swallow
some soup, and after a hot bath she fell into bed and
slept dreamlessly until morning.

She certainly felt more rested, but a dreadful feeling
of failure still clung to her like mist. She was hanging
around the hotel lobby looking at the occasional snow-
flake which drifted gently out of the iron-grey sky when
Maggy came looking for her.

'Luc wants you, honey,' she said. 'He's in Chalet 10.'

Heart beating, Ashley grabbed her parka and made
for the door. 'Thanks Maggy.' She hoped she had managed to disguise the dread that overshadowed her at his
summons.

Chalet 10 was shuttered and dark. It had been turned
into a makeshift projection room so that Lucas could
view the rushes. Straight chairs had been lined up before
a portable screen, and Lucas sat on one with his long legs
thrust out before him. There was no one else in the
room.

'Ah, there you are, Ashley. Come on in, I want you to
see this.' He looked exhausted, his dark eyes shadowed,
the lines on his face etched harshly.

Silently she sat on the chair furthest away from him.
She wanted to cry at the sight of his tired face. She

longed to comfort him, but knew this was not possible.

He started the machine which whirred for a moment. Then there was an image of the slate and yesterday's two-shot came on the screen.

It was the first time Ashley had ever seen herself on any kind of screen, and she was horrified. Surely this mouthing, posturing creature had nothing to do with her! Compared to Sloane, who was so still and quiet, she looked like a take-off from a silent movie. Except that this was sound and she bellowed out of all proportion.

Mercifully it soon came to an end, and Lucas turned off the projector. Ashley sat staring blindly at the blank screen, her lashes starred with tears of mortification.

Lucas broke the agonising silence. 'Well, what do you think?'

'It's . . . I'm terrible . . . I had no idea . . .' Her voice cracked ignominiously.

Lucas pulled a Kleenex tissue from his pocket and handed it to her. 'I didn't show you this because I wanted to hurt you, Ashley,' he said, 'but I thought that if I showed you the actual results you might understand what I mean by—too big.'

'Yes, I do now,' she gulped.

'I can't use much of yesterday's footage, you realise that?'

She didn't trust herself to speak. She merely looked at him mutely, her grey eyes rimmed with tears.

'I'll have to use the shots of Sloane for the major part of the scene,' he continued, 'which is a pity, because the focus should really be on Elizabeth.'

Ashley found her voice again. 'Are you trying to break it to me gently that . . . that I'm fired,' she asked shakily.

His voice was as steely as a dagger. 'Is that what you want?' he said contemptuously. 'To quit? I didn't think you were a coward.'

'I'm not.' Stung, she scrunched the Kleenex into a soggy ball and dropped it into the waste-basket. 'But if it's hopeless . . .'

'I didn't say it was hopeless. Stop jumping to conclusions. I believe that you have it in you to be a first-class film actress . . .'

'I have?' Her tear-stained eyes widened with astonishment—and hope.

'But only if you'll learn to *listen*. Not just to me, but to the scene itself, rather than just saying the words.'

'I thought I *was* doing that,' she insisted.

'The hell you were!' He turned on her like a tiger. 'You fought me all day, Ashley. Everything I suggested—you did the opposite. Your damned stubbornness cost us a precious day's work!'

'I'm sorry.' She was genuinely contrite.

'And you'll do what I tell you for a change?' His eyes were like a laser-beam.

She nodded. 'I'll do what you tell me.'

'*Right!* Then today and tomorrow we shoot only scenes without dialogue. Then on our day off I'll give you a crash course in film acting technique.'

'*You* will?'

'*I* will. Do you agree?' He fixed her with a look.

She lowered her eyes humbly. 'I agree.'

'No dates on your day off. No skylarking off with Tim for cosy dinners.'

Ashley was about to protest at his high-handedness, but thought better of it and merely nodded her head in obedience.

'Good girl!' Lucas tweaked one of her braids—she had plaited her hair into two braids, since it was now so dirty it was becoming unmanageable. 'Get into the jeep. I'll drive you to work.'

She trotted to the jeep meekly enough, but her spirit was returning, and she knew that maintaining this air of submission was going to be difficult.

Lucas had her well and truly in a corner. She *had* to toe the line if she wanted to keep the job. And she wanted the job desperately. Also he had hit a nerve when he had accused her of being a quitter. For quitting was something she utterly despised. She was determined to beat this problem, to learn camera techniques, and to show him . . . and herself . . . that she could do it. She resigned herself to accepting Lucas's authority without an argument, at least until she had conquered this particular hurdle. These thoughts occupied her as they drove silently to Tremblant Park.

By the time they were ready to shoot it had started to snow heavily—much to Lucas's delight. This was the weather he needed for his long shots of Ashley, frightened and lost in the forest.

For the rest of the day she pushed and struggled her way through waist-deep snow. Snow that was thick yet loose-packed, like icy swansdown. The great trees swayed and creaked, and the snow fell in the wind surging towards her. It was like being in the centre of one of those glass paperweights, the kind you shake and the snowflakes fly—except that this snow was fine as crystal grit that stung her face and clogged her collar with brittle granules.

The cold was ferocious, and within an hour she was numb and shivering. Her boots and long skirt were soaked, and her hair was caked with half-frozen snow. But she was resolved to be stoical. She suspected this was a test for her after yesterday's debacle and she was determined not to falter.

She had reached a point of frigid agony, when every movement was an effort, when the panic she was supposed to be acting was a natural part of her and she didn't need to act at all, when the cameraman shouted to them to cut the scene because the camera had frozen.

Lucas squinted at the lowering sky. 'We've practically no light left anyway, Steve,' he said. 'Let's call it a wrap and get a really early start tomorrow. Providing it goes on snowing, of course. What's the latest weather forecast, Maggy?' She told him that it was supposed to snow for at least twenty-four hours. 'Good! We'll start as soon as it's light.' His face was stung to a dark hue of reddish-brown by the cold. The hood of his fur-lined parka was up, but a few jet-black curls fell, wet and shining, on his broad forehead. The rest of the crew looked pinched and miserable, but Lucas seemed to be in his element here in the storm-tossed forest. His high cheekbones gleamed, and Ashley could see in his face more clearly than ever his proud Indian heritage.

Her fingers were so frozen she had to have assistance in unlacing her boots and unbuttoning her costume. Dressed in her own clothes at last, she was driven back to the hotel, huddled in her snow-suit, chilled to her fragile bones.

It was only after a long hot soak in the tub that she began to feel the warmth tingling back into her body.

She had just put on her turquoise Viyella dressing-gown and was wondering if she had the energy to dress and go up the hill to the hotel for dinner, when there was a rap at her door. Holding the gown tightly around her, she opened the door a crack and peered out. Lucas, balancing a large tray, stood on the threshold.

'Lucas! What on earth . . . ?'

'I've brought you some food,' he said, 'which may crash at your feet if you don't let me in—it's heavy!'

Dazed, Ashley opened the door and he entered, depositing the tray on the table.

'I was just about to get dressed and go to the dining-room,' she protested, very aware of the fact that she was naked beneath the clinging gown. From the admiring look in Lucas's black eyes he was aware of it too.

'Well, I've saved you the trouble, haven't I?' he said. 'It's a reward for being a real pro. Today was very tough.'

The knowledge that she had pleased him did more to warm her than anything so far.

'But I warn you, tomorrow's going to be tougher,' he went on, 'and I want you to eat your dinner like a good girl, and then go straight to bed. I need you on the set at dawn.' He uncovered a bowl of soup with a flourish and draped a napkin over his arm. '*Madame est servie!*' He pulled out her chair.

Joy at being with him mingled with fear at the intimacy this situation created. The familiar dinner, her déshabillée. Just two days ago she'd sworn not to let this happen again . . . but . . . she'd promised not to argue.

'Lucas, I . . . I don't know what to say . . .'

'How about—"Thank you very much for being so thoughtful, Luc"?'

Gently he pushed her into the chair and laid the napkin over her lap. His eyes lingered at the shadowy hollow between her firm young breasts, and when he spoke again his voice was husky. With an effort he controlled himself and said, 'Now you eat your nice hot soup before it gets cold. There are lamb chops to follow. And a jug of cocoa, not coffee. I want you to sleep. Now I must get back to the hotel.'

'To . . to the hotel?'

'Mmm—for dinner. Sloane's waiting for me.'

This caused ice to form round her heart.

'Now remember, Ashley—straight to bed after your meal. Promise?'

'If I have the energy to stagger there.' She picked up her spoon and tasted the soup. It was mushroom . . . one of her favourites. 'Thank you very much for being so thoughtful, Luc,' she said, dismissing him.

'Not at all.' He stood in the doorway, his tall frame huge in the padded parka, his black hair tumbling across his tanned forehead. 'It was a rough day,' he said again. 'You did well.'

And my reward's dinner in my room alone after you've leered down my dressing-gown, Ashley thought with acerbity. She continued eating her soup. With her back towards him she waved goodbye with her spare hand. She heard her door slam, and she was alone.

She knew she was being unreasonable to feel slighted because he had gone back to have dinner with Sloane— particularly since her first reaction on opening the door and seeing him had been one of alarm, but nevertheless she felt let down. She was back on that emotional see-saw again, and she seemed unable to control it.

As Lucas had warned her, the next day's filming was long and hard. For one thing the weather was worse. The wind raged through the forest like a wild animal, and the snowfall was now of blizzard proportions. Ashley stum-

bled and fought her way through snowdrifts, fell into
snow-filled ditches, and her hair and clothes were ripped
and torn on branches and in dense bush. Lucas was
intensely happy about the whole day and seemed imper-
vious to the weather.

Sloane joined them after lunch, staying in her car
close by until absolutely necessary, then sulkily doing
her scenes in the punishing cold.

'Luc is really *too* much,' she muttered to Ashley. 'I
mean, darling! Realism's all very well, but he does go
overboard!'

Ashley didn't know how Sloane managed it, but even
under these harsh conditions she managed to look glamorous. When her hair was whipped by the wind it
streamed out like a black silk cloud, while Ashley's was
now so badly in need of a shampoo it lay tangled and
matted on her dirt-streaked face. There was blood on
her face too. A bramble had scratched her, but when
Jane had tried to wipe the blood away Lucas had stopped
her.

'Leave it!' he had barked. 'The dirtier and worse she
looks the better!'

Ashley noted wryly that even Sloane's nose didn't run
in the cold the way hers did. Still she doggedly went on
with the work in hand in spite of all the discomfort, for
she found herself beginning to enjoy this work. She was
being physically challenged to the full. Now if she could
do something positive about the rest of her performance, all would be well. When they wrapped later that
afternoon she was freezing, tired, but also filled with
satisfaction. She'd done it! She'd got through the day
without a whimper of complaint, and a minimum of
takes.

Arriving back at the hotel she found a note from Tim
waiting for her. 'Hi, beautiful!' she read. 'I had planned
to take you dancing tonight, but that slavedriver Luc has
sent me to Toronto on a million errands and I won't be
back for at least twenty-four hours. I guess the dancing
will have to wait. Love, Tim.'

She wondered if Lucas had invented all those errands

to get Tim out of the way. If he was afraid she would have gone out dancing rather than resting ready for tomorrow's drama lesson he needn't have worried. After nine hours floundering about in snowdrifts she was in no shape to go anywhere, except bed.

She ate at the company table and sensed that for the first time since she had joined them the crew accepted her. Not that they had been unfriendly before, but now there was a subtle change in their attitude. They teased her more, and called her by her own name rather than the name of the character she was playing, a sure sign of belonging.

Lucas sat at the centre of the long table with Ashley on one side, Sloane on the other. The torrid star was clearly in a bad temper. She sent things back to the kitchen, moaned about how tired she was, and glared at the assembled company through slitted eyes, her mouth square with discontent. Ashley heard her mutter to Lucas.

'Honestly, darling! I did think we might go out some-where else to eat. It's not as if we have to work tomor-row.'

'*I* have to work tomorrow.' Lucas poured cream over his apple pie. 'So does Ashley.'

'Oh, really?' Sloane sounded caustic. 'Doing *what*, may I ask?'

'Well, it's really none of your business, Sloane,' he was quite genial, 'but I want to work on some scenes with her. Prepare her for next week's shoot.'

'I don't deny she needs it,' Sloane said nastily, 'but on our day off, darling! It really does mess things up.'

'Not for you it doesn't. We didn't have any plans for tomorrow.' He attacked his pie with gusto.

'But *Luc*! The deBoers are staying at L'Esterel. They've asked me over for the day and I said I'd bring you.'

'First I've heard of it, Sloane,' he pointed out. 'Any-way, you know I can't make plans to socialise when I'm working.'

She got up from the table with a face like thunder.

'You are turning into a very *dull and boring* workaholic!' she spat at him.

'Then you won't miss me tomorrow, will you?' He pushed aside his empty plate with a sigh of satisfaction. 'That was great apple pie,' he said. 'You should have had some.'

With an exclamation of annoyance Sloane turned on her heel and left the dining-room.

Unruffled, Lucas poured himself some coffee from the pot before him. 'By the way, Ashley,' he said, 'I'm sure you'll be glad to hear that you can now wash your hair. You don't need to look quite so bedraggled for the rest of the shoot.'

'Then I think I'll say goodnight now and fling myself in the shower. I've a feeling getting my hair clean again is going to take some time.' She rose and prepared to leave.

'About tomorrow,' Lucas said. 'Be in the main lobby at nine and bring your script. OK?' He was totally impersonal.

'OK! Goodnight, everyone!' and picking up her hand-bag Ashley left the room.

She was crossing the parking lot on the way to her chalet when Sloane hailed her from her car. The storm had ceased and the fresh snow glittered in the lights along the drive.

Ashley looked down into the car at Sloane's beautiful, ill-humoured face. 'Ashley, I just want to warn you,' she said.

'Warn me?' Ashley's smooth brow crinkled with surprise.

'Yes. About this . . . *work* with Luc tomorrow. Don't let it go to your head.'

A frisson of irritation tightened Ashley's well-formed lips. 'Being in need of coaching is hardly a reason for conceit.'

'Well, you just remember that, *darling*.' The star's rough voice was laced with venom. 'We wouldn't want to get above ourselves, would we?' She jabbed the accelerator and skidded out of the parking lot at top speed, showering Ashley with a spray of snow, and leaving the astonished girl watching the red tail-lights of her car disappear into the night.

CHAPTER SEVEN

ASHLEY was in the lobby of the hotel well before nine the following morning, but Lucas was there before her. He looked very elegant in a pair of dove-grey suede slacks teamed with a navy Fair Isle sweater. The collar of his grey flannel shirt was open, exposing the strong column of his throat.

He looked at her approvingly. 'Morning, Red. You're early. Is that because you're keen, or because you want to get it over with?'

'You make a drama lesson sound like a visit to the dentist!' She brushed back a stray curl from her smooth cheek. She had washed her hair and wore it loose. It swung around her shoulders in glossy chestnut waves.

'Should have worn my white coat,' he teased. 'Talking of coats, do you have yours?'

Ashley indicated the tweed coat over her arm. Since she was shampooed and manicured this morning she had decided to wear a dress for a change of pace from the eternal jeans and parka. Aunt Constance had provided her with a warm shirt-dress of heather-coloured tweed. She had knotted a lilac scarf round her throat, and emphasised her eyes with a trace of mauve shadow. It felt nice to know she was looking good again.

'Great!' Lucas pulled on his sheepskin coat and helped her into her tweed one. 'We'll take one of the station wagons—warmer than the jeep. And we'll stop in the village for groceries.'

'Groceries?' What on earth was he talking about?

'Mmm—for lunch. Acting lessons always make me hungry.'

'Can't we eat lunch here?'

'Oh, we're not staying here to work,' he informed her in his charming offhand manner. 'I'm taking you to Hackmatack.'

'Where on earth's that?' she queried.

'It's our family place twenty miles north of here. Hackmatack is the Algonquin name for tamarack tree.'

By now they were outside, Lucas guiding her purposefully to the parking lot. The sky was a heavy grey again, but there was no wind. It felt as if the morning was holding its breath.

'Why do we have to leave Tremblant for this lesson?' Ashley protested. Part of her wasn't at all sure she wanted to go speeding off twenty miles into the bush with Lucas. The other part of her was filled with tremulous anticipation.

Adroitly he manoeuvred her into the car and closed her door. 'Several reasons,' he said. 'First: I don't want countless interruptions, and that would be bound to happen at the hotel.' He started the engine and sat back, waiting for the car to warm up. 'Second: it *is* your day off, and even though you have to work, it'll be a break for you to get away for a few hours. Third: I thought you might enjoy Hackmatack. Give you a chance to see a genuine old Quebec country house. And fourth . . .' He put the car in gear and drove out of the hotel grounds.

'Fourth?' she questioned when he didn't continue.

He gave her a sphinx-like smile. 'I'll tell you the fourth reason another time,' he said.

They stopped at a fashionable grocery store in the village and Lucas proceeded to fill a wicker basket with tins and packets. He seemed in a holiday humour rather than a working one, and whistled softly under his breath as he strode down the well stocked aisles of the store.

He checked over the basket. 'Bread, lobster soup, eggs, cheese, sardines, cookies, olives—oh, and we must have some of their pâté, it's famous. And some cream, and a tin of fruit. What kind do you like?'

'I would *kill* for tinned apricots. But honestly, Lucas, you've got enough there for a month!' Ashley giggled. 'We don't need all that!'

'We can leave what we don't eat for my papa. He'll polish it off, don't worry.' And laden with provisions they drove into the mountains.

Even the lowering skies, dark with foreboding, could not rob the scenery of its beauty. The forests were a dramatic green-black, touched here and there with a slash of pale silver-grey where the trunk of a birch tree broke through the dark foliage of firs. Often Ashley could glimpse an expanse of smooth shimmering white; a frozen lake now several feet deep in fresh snow, the only marks on it the tracks of deer, and rabbit, and fox.

Looking at the ancient landscape, so majestic in its frozen splendour, she felt a surge of emotion, for in that instant she knew with complete certainty that she had fallen in love, not only with Lucas, but with his country too. She was irrevocably bound to the vastness of this lonely land, even if she would never see it again when her work here was finished.

They turned off the main road onto a freshly ploughed track. A sign, bearing the name 'Martineaux' under a painting of a tamarack tree, pointed to the valley below.

'We're lucky, Leduc's already ploughed our road,' Lucas remarked.

'Leduc?'

'A local farmer. We've had an arrangement with him for years. He keeps our road open in the winter. But sometimes he doesn't get around to it till later.'

They started to descend a fairly steep slope. The trees thinned, and below them they could see a lake, frozen and white, and the roof of a large old house which stood on the cleared ground near the lake-front. They drove into a space at the back of the house and came to a halt.

Ashley climbed out of the car into a silent, crystal world. It was so still after the noise of the car she thought she could hear herself breathe. The air felt cold and dry; she could almost taste it, like sparkling wine. It intoxicated her with its purity, and she wanted to sing aloud, she felt so exuberant.

Lucas plugged the car into a block heater so the engine wouldn't freeze. Then he unlocked the backdoor, and handing her one of the bags of groceries led her into the house.

Despite the overcast sky it was bright inside. Hackmatack was an old house that was made of wood, the inside walls painted white. The kitchen, where they deposited their supplies, was large and comfortable. There were the usual modern American conveniences—refriger- ator, electric stove, and a large freezer—but these had clearly been added during the years, for there was also a wood-stove, an old-fashioned stone sink, and oil lamps as well as electric light.

'Bit chill in here,' said Lucas, turning up the thermo- stat. 'I'll light the stove, that should warm us up. Then we'll do a tour of the house.'

Ashley helped him unpack the food. Then, still wear- ing their overcoats for warmth, he took her through the rooms. The kitchen overlooked the back of the moun- tain and the track leading to the main road, but the living area overlooked a sloping sweep of lawn and the lake. At one end of the immense room stood an enormous round dining-table of polished maple. She counted twelve dining chairs around it. Against the wall stood a tall dresser, its shelves filled with handsome blue and white antique china. The planked wooden floor was bare in the dining area and painted soft grey-blue, a colour that was picked up in the large Turkish carpet that lay in the other part of the room. Before a fireplace, that looked large enough to roast an ox, stood various wicker chairs and matching sofas, all painted the same shade as the floor, with cushioned seats of glazed cotton in a faded yellow, white, and pink floral design. There were bookshelves overflowing with every kind of book, from fairy stories to a treatise on Transcultural Psychiatry.

Photographs in silver or soft Morocco leather frames stood on the mantelpiece and on various occasional tables. They showed groups of people—family, Ashley supposed—at winter and summer activities. People on skis, or seated on toboggans, smiled out at her. Groups of swimmers, crews of sailboats, children holding up the day's catch of fish. She was particularly intrigued by a photo of a younger Lucas wearing swim trunks, his body bronzed and muscular, his arm around a smiling dark- haired girl.

'That's my sister, Marie-André,' he said. He picked up a leather-framed portrait. 'And this is Papa. I took it in Montreal last year.'

The photo showed a fine, hawk-like face, framed with abundant silver hair. Lucas had his sloe-black eyes, his craggy face, and the same uncompromising arrogant stare.

He applied a match to the fire that was laid in the cavernous fireplace. 'Let's get this started so it'll be nice and warm for work,' he said, 'then I'll show you the upstairs.'

'How is it all the fires are waiting to be lit?' Ashley asked, suspicious. It was beginning to look as if this spur of the moment visit had been elaborately planned.

'Madame Leduc. She comes in twice a week and keeps things in order. Been doing it for years.' The kindling of driftwood and twigs spurted to life with a flare of orange flame. Lucas replaced the brass fireguard and led the way up the shallow staircase. The walls were unpainted in this part of the house and glowed with a satiny patina.

There were twelve bedrooms, furnished simply but very comfortably. White woven curtains hung at the windows, contrasting pleasantly against the warm wooden walls. All the beds had handmade quilts of different designs.

'My mother used to collect antique quilts for Hackmatack,' he explained. He opened a door at the far end of the corridor. 'This is my room now. I graduated from one of the smaller ones when I left college.'

This room was the next in size after the master bedroom, which his father still occupied. It had two large windows overlooking the lake. Bookshelves ran from floor to ceiling of one alcove. Hand-braided rugs in shades of red and blue lay on the polished floor. There was also a fireplace, smaller than the huge one downstairs, flanked by chintz-covered armchairs. But dominating the entire room was a massive fourposter bed covered in a scarlet and white quilt.

'Nice, eh?' He looked at her quizzically. 'Believe me,

once you've climbed into that bed it's hard to climb out again!' His eyes were bold with sensual invitation. He nodded in the direction of the fireplace. 'Madame Leduc's laid the fire,' he said softly, 'all I have to do is put a match to it. Then it's the coziest room in the house, believe me, Ashley.'

'I believe you.' She forced herself to sound matter-of-fact in spite of the blush that was burning her cheeks. 'Shouldn't we be getting to work, Lucas? The morning will be gone.'

'Is this haste a thirst for knowledge? Or do bedrooms confuse you?' he mocked.

'I'm not the least confused,' she said, in the face of all evidence to the contrary. 'Should I be?'

The mocking glint died in his eyes. 'I don't know, Red,' he said, 'I never know with you. I still haven't figured you out.' He put his arm across her shoulders and started guiding her downstairs again.

She trod carefully on the wide slippery stairs, for she had taken off her boots at the kitchen entrance and was in her stockinged feet. She was wearing purple ribbed-wool tights, and they slid alarmingly on the shiny painted surface. Twice she would have fallen if Lucas hadn't had his arm around her. Each time he held her close she thought she could feel his heart thudding against his ribs, but always she quickly regained her balance and gently pushed him away, so she couldn't be sure.

Back in the living room she managed to put distance between them by curling up with her script on one of the wicker chairs. Lucas strode around the room. He seemed filled with nervous energy. Fiddling with the photographs and ornaments, and drumming his long fingers in a rapid tattoo on the mantel.

'The secret of acting in front of the camera,' he said at last, 'is to remember that it's like a magnifying glass. It can show an audience things that are impossible on stage. Film deals primarily with emotions, not words. On film I can show what the quiver of an eyelid can reveal, what's meant by the twitch of a finger. All you need to do, Ashley, is understand the character and the scene inside your head, and the camera will record what you're feeling.'

He suddenly knelt at her feet, putting his hands on the arms of her chair, imprisoning her. 'You not only have one of the most beautiful faces I've ever seen,' he said, his voice low and husky, 'it's also one of the most expressive. I want to capture the thoughts behind those wonderful grey eyes of yours. I want to photograph the flush of colour that ebbs and flows in your face.' He traced the curve of her cheek with his finger, causing her heart to race. 'You could act a whole film without dialogue,' he whispered, 'the flutter of your lashes, the curve of your mouth. The way you look at me now, so . . .' He dropped his hands and got swiftly to his feet again, his manner suddenly terse and businesslike.

'We'll work on scene twenty-five,' he said crisply. 'Don't use your hands, and take time to think before you say any lines. I want to *see* the emotion in your face, not listen to the words.'

The change in him was so startling Ashley had trouble adjusting. But she should have guessed, she reflected, *anything* he said to her, even the most persuasive compliment, was for one reason and one reason only—to get a performance out of her for his film. Like all film people his work seemed to be his entire life. Nothing else appeared to exist for him. Any attraction she might have he saw only in terms of his film, his camera, and she would be a fool to imagine otherwise. She must remember that tenderness from him was a weapon, a means to an end, a way to coax the performance he wanted from her. Nothing more.

They worked for two hours—hard, concentrated work. This time Ashley did not fight Lucas's direction and did what he asked. The magic started to work. She found she could summon up her emotions and give him genuine fear when he commanded it, could weep, could flush with happiness, or grow pale with sorrow. She found herself longing to test her new-found skill before the camera tomorrow, to prove to him that she had mastered her new art.

At length he called a halt to the lesson. 'That's enough for today, Red.' He took her script from her. 'You see?' he teased. 'You can be a very apt pupil when you co-operate.' He searched her face. 'Are you as quick to learn other lessons, I wonder?'

She answered him coolly, 'It depends what the subject is.'

'*Thrift* might be a good one for you,' was his cutting rejoinder. Then seeing her glow with irritation at this gibe, he said, 'It's too nice a day for lectures, Red. Let's go for a walk before lunch to blow the cobwebs away.'

She looked out at the expanse of smooth white snow. 'A walk? Isn't the snow too deep for walking?'

'We have snow-shoes in the garage . . . or toboggans. Have you ever coasted on a toboggan?' Ashley shook her titian head. 'Then prepare yourself for a new experience.' He bustled away and reappeared with a fur-lined jacket. 'One of Marie-André's old ones. She left it here for guests. Your coat won't be warm enough.'

She pulled on the jacket—it was much too big, but warm and snug—and waited outside the garage, looking up at the sky which was now almost purple and hung low on the surrounding mountains.

Lucas joined her pulling two toboggans behind him and they set off up the ploughed road to a hill he said he had always played on as a child.

He had undergone another of his rapid changes of mood and was now like a small boy on holiday. His air of boisterous fun was infectious, and Ashley found it impossible to remain aloof and guarded. She skipped along beside him, dragging her toboggan, kicking the snow with the toe of her boot, and feeling happier than she ever remembered feeling in her life.

Lucas pointed out animal tracks in the snow, told her the names of trees and birds and how, as a boy, he had found an injured Saw-whet owl—no bigger than a teacup—and nursed it back to health.

They climbed the ploughed road to the crest of the

hill, then turned into the meadow. 'I'll go ahead and beat a path for you,' he said. 'Just walk in my footsteps.'

'Like Good King Wenceslas' page,' she laughed.

He turned to face her, his expression unexpectedly grave. 'Don't mistake me for a saint, Red. I'm not one—be warned.'

'Your footprints certainly aren't warm,' Ashley replied, keeping the conversation deliberately light-hearted. 'If I have to stand still on this hill much longer I'll turn into an icicle!'

Lucas looked at her searchingly for a moment, then adopted her bantering tone. 'OK, Red. This is the run. Sit on your toboggan and I'll give you a push.' He brushed the fluffy, dry snow off the padded seat, and when she had settled herself comfortably he thrust her down the hill.

The flat-bottomed toboggan sped down the silver-smooth hill with a gentle whooshing sound, and the cold wind turned her cheeks a rosy pink and made her eyes sparkle. When she slowed to a halt at the bottom of the hill she let out a loud war-whoop of delight and started ploughing her way up the hill again, dragging her toboggan behind her. Lucas skimmed down the hill and coasted in an arc at her feet.

'You liked that, Red?'

'I loved it! I'm going to do it again. Let's toboggan for *hours*, Lucas!'

'You're going to be pretty tired if we climb up and down this hill for *hours*,' he chuckled, 'but we'll keep going for a while. Let's walk up on the road, though. It's easier.'

He kicked a path through the deep powdery snow to the road, then they climbed the hill again, and again she sped down the slope, shrieking with pleasure, like a little girl on a merry-go-round.

She became quite adept with her toboggan, twisting and turning on the icy descent as he did. After several runs Lucas patted some snow into a mound near the bottom of the hill.

'What are you doing?' she asked.

'You're getting so good I figure it's time to give you a bit of a challenge,' he replied. 'This will act as a jump at the bottom of the run.'

'Great! Let's try it.' Ashley started climbing up the hill. She was now as warm as toast and radiant.

'I'll go first,' said Lucas, 'so you can see how I handle the toboggan when I hit the bump.' He kicked himself off and sped down the hill, his scarlet scarf streaming out behind him. When he hit the mound of snow his toboggan rose up into the air briefly, then shot down the rest of the hill at double speed.

Ashley pushed hard to get herself going really fast and flew down the hill like a red-crowned bird. The rushing air felt icy against her glowing cheeks. Her toboggan hit the bump at the top speed, then she lost control, she and her craft parted company, and she landed head first in a nearby snowbank. She reappeared, gasping for breath and helpless with laughter. Her toque had fallen off, and her hair was a tangle of tawny curls. She blinked to free her long lashes from a frosting of snowflakes.

'Ashley! Sweetheart, are you all right?' Lucas fought his way through the deep snow and knelt beside her, his face filled with concern. 'Honey, are you all right?'

'I . . . I think so,' she said through her laughter.

'I should never have built that dumb jump,' he went on. 'If you'd hurt yourself . . . !' His black brows were creased with worry.

Ashley sat up in the soft snow. 'The only thing that's hurt is my dignity,' she said. She shook the snow out of her hair and smiled up at him.

He leaned forward, and cupping her heart-shaped face in his hands kissed her gently on the mouth. His lips felt warm and dry. This time he didn't try to force her mouth to yield under his, but was infinitely tender. After a brief flicker of resistance Ashley sighed and trustingly gave herself to the voluptuous pleasure of his kiss.

Finally he released her. 'You're so lovely. Even Good King Wenceslas would kiss you if he saw you now,' he murmured.

Caution suddenly stirred in Ashley. What was she

doing? She was supposed to be on her guard! She clambered on to her feet and brushed herself down.

'I certainly wish the old boy was around now,' she said over-brightly. 'I could use a few warm footprints. It's getting very chill.' She lowered her eyes to hide the fact that, in spite of all her caution, she was filled with a wild happiness because he had kissed her so lovingly.

'It's going to snow again,' Lucas said. He sounded subdued. He tucked her hand in his, and pulling the toboggans behind them they returned to the house.

While Lucas was upstairs putting on dry slacks—his suede ones were soaking wet from the snow—Ashley heated lobster soup in the kitchen. She had refused his offer of a dressing-gown while she dried the hem of her dress, preferring to let it flap damply round her legs rather than remove any garments while he was around. Sharing lunch while wearing one of his dressing-gowns seemed a little too intimate for safety.

They ate at the long pine kitchen table. After the soup they picnicked on French bread and pâté, and shared a tin of sardines. They drank Moselle that was the colour of winter sunshine and fizzed slightly in the tall cut-crystal wine glasses.

'That was delicious,' said Ashley, pushing away her crumb-strewn plate and sighing with content. 'I love impromptu meals.'

'What do you mean, impromptu?' Lucas reverted to his familiar teasing manner. He had been unusually silent since their kiss. 'I worked like a slave planning which cans to open! And speaking of cans, we mustn't forget your apricots.'

'I couldn't, Luc! I'm too full of sardines and pâté. Besides, I'll get fat.' She patted her trim waist. 'You don't want a fat Elizabeth in your film, do you?'

'You're not the type to gain weight, my dear,' he said, his dark eyes appraising, 'but I won't insist. We'll have them later, to give us energy for the drive back. And now I'm going to build up the fire in the other room, and we'll relax after our meal.'

He left her while she cleared the table and made them

instant coffee. The idea of resting after their energetic morning appealed to her, but her alarm-system was on alert now, so it was with some misgivings that she carried the pretty enamelled tray of coffee into the living room.

Lucas turned from poking the fire and took the tray from her. 'I suggest you put your feet up on that,' he indicated one of the sofas, 'and have a snooze. You've put in quite a morning.'

'I *never* sleep during the day,' she said firmly, not adding that she considered it far too dangerous to lie asleep on a sofa with him around. She was irrationally disappointed when he didn't insist.

'Suit yourself, Red,' he said. 'I may doze a bit, though, so don't wake me.'

He stretched his long lean body on the sofa and picked up a section of the newspaper that was lying on the floor by his side. 'I picked up the *New York Times* this morning. Do you want the entertainment section?'

'I'd prefer world affairs, thank you,' she said, irritated that he would assume her interests were limited by the theatre.

He raised a seismographic eyebrow. 'Are you on the level?'

'Certainly.'

'Then you sure don't run true to type.'

'To type?' she queried.

'Actress-type people don't usually want to know about world affairs,' he explained. 'However, there is one item in the entertainments section that may be of interest.' He handed her the paper. 'It's the cover story.'

Ashley looked at the headline: 'NEW YORK'S CENTURY THEATRE CONFIRMS CANADIAN LUCAS MARTINEAUX TO DIRECT *KING LEAR*,' she read. Hastily she scanned the article. It was true! Lucas would be directing *Lear*, which would open in New York next autumn. Speechless with surprise, she put the paper down.

'Well?' He was looking at her through half-closed eyes.

'*Shakespeare*'s *King Lear*?'

'None other.'

She struggled to find the right words. 'You mean . . . on . . . on *stage*?'

'On stage. Yes.' His voice was neutral.

'B-but I . . . I thought . . . but you're a *film* director!'

'And you're *damned insulting*!' He was on his feet in one swift movement. 'And you have the unmitigated gall to call *me* prejudiced! For your information, I have worked for the theatre before, *and* been successful.' His flinty eyes shot sparks of anger. 'I did think that maybe . . . *maybe* . . . you were starting to lose that snobbish attitude you have towards us "film slobs".'

'I have . . . I mean . . .'

He ignored her and started pacing the floor, the fire lighting his face with red shadows, making him look demonic in his fury. 'But *no*! You make it quite plain that as far as you're concerned no mere film director is capable of tackling the Bard—let alone on *stage*!'

He glanced down at her, and she realised that his anger was a mask, and behind it he was deeply wounded. She got up too, since she felt at a distinct disadvantage when he towered over her like that.

'Lucas . . . I didn't mean to hurt your feelings . . .'

'My feelings aren't hurt,' he grated.

'Then why are you so upset?' A long silence followed.

'Don't be so bloody reasonable,' he said at last with the ghost of a smile.

'It came out all wrong,' Ashley explained. 'You took me by surprise. I'm delighted for you, and I know you'll be great—really!' Impulsively she caught his hands in hers. Her eyes were wide with fervour. She hated seeing him hurt like this. And to have been the cause, no matter how unwittingly, was unbearable. 'I'm learning so much since I've started working on *Time of Trial*. I've *certainly* learnt that acting for the movies isn't easy!' She gave a wry chuckle. 'I even need special coaching! And as for thinking of film people in terms of being "slobs" . . . that couldn't be further from the truth. I like you . . . you all . . . so much. Steve . . . and Maggy . . .'

'And Tim?' Lucas's eyes were like black coals in his drawn face. 'Do you like Tim too?'

'Y-yes, I like him.'

He let out a shuddering sigh and gently released his hands. Turning to look down into the fire, he asked softly, 'Are you in love with him?'

'In *love* with Tim? Not in the least,' she answered evenly. Oh, if only you guessed! she thought, gazing at the base of his neck, which looked vulnerable, like the neck of a small boy, at this angle.

'Well, I suggest you keep it that way.' Lucas turned to face her again his face drained of emotion. 'It's never a good idea to mix business with pleasure. Take my advice and avoid it.'

Ashley was tempted to point out that his alleged relationship with Sloane seemed a pretty good mixture of business and pleasure, but she decided to keep quiet. One argument an hour was all she could handle with Lucas Martineaux.

He sat back in his wicker sofa and handed her a section of newspaper. 'Here you are, Red. World affairs—the bit you wanted in the first place.' He buried himself in his own paper, making it quite clear that the discussion was closed.

Ashley stretched out again and tried to read, but she found it impossible to concentrate. She disliked any kind of deceit. When Lucas had asked her if she was in love with Tim it would have been so easy to have told him the truth, particularly with the memory of his gentle kiss still fresh on her lips. But she couldn't. Not if he and Sloane were lovers. There was no point in being fooled by his kiss either. It probably meant no more to him than a moment of fun with a pretty girl. If she was unwise enough to let him know how she cherished that kiss it would merely prove to him that yet another female had fallen under his spell—and that was a role she had no intention of playing.

She gave up on the newspaper and lay staring into the fire. She was feeling very drowsy, and her eyelids drooped. I'll just close my eyes for a few seconds, she thought, and then I must rouse myself.

The clinking of tea-cups woke her. She was now covered with a red mohair rug, light as a cloud. Lucas must have tucked it round her small body as she slept. The room was now dim and shadowy, for the fire had burned low and was a rosy pile of embers.

He wheeled the tea trolley to the end of her sofa. 'Teatime, Red!' he said.

Ashley sat up guiltily. 'How long have I been asleep?'

'About two hours.' Lucas threw another log on the fire and switched on a table lamp. 'Not bad for a girl who never sleeps during the day.' He had changed back into his suede slacks and looked fresh and combed and alert.

'You should have woken me,' she protested, running her fingers through her tousled red curls and blinking her eyes rapidly in an effort to come to.

'Why? You needed a rest. Don't be so guilt-ridden. Anyway, there's no rush. We can't leave yet, as you'll see for yourself if you look out of the window.'

'What do you . . . ?' She crossed to the windows and looked at the lake—except that there was no lake to be seen—a wall of white snow pressed against the panes. Even the dark trees at the end of the clearing were invisible. She now realised that the gloom was not the twilight as she had supposed, but was this curtain of snow blocking out the light.

She turned back to Lucas, her eyes wide. 'Is it a blizzard?'

'Nope! It's a white-out. Happens sometimes when it gets very cold. We'll just stay put until it lifts.'

'Stay put? You mean . . . not go back to the hotel?' Apprehension made her well-modulated voice shrill.

He smiled ironically. 'Don't get into a panic, Ashley. It shouldn't last more than a couple of hours. But we're not driving back in a white-out. That would be absolute madness. So come and pour the tea like a sensible girl and quit worrying.'

She came back to the fireside and did as he suggested. After all, she reasoned, he wasn't responsible for the weather conditions, and it was still quite early. Besides, it was cosy drinking tea in front of the fire with Lucas, the world outside obliterated and forgotten. He put a record on the stereo—Mahler's Fourth Symphony—and the lush, impassioned music flooded the room, while the golden flames burnished her sorrel-hued hair.

By the time the record came to an end it was dark and they decided to forage for dinner. While Lucas made up the dying fire again, Ashley, wrapped in an apron she found hanging on the kitchen door, made cheese omelettes.

They ate before the fire, where Lucas toasted the remains of their French bread, spearing thick slices on an old-fashioned toasting-fork, the sprinkling of dark hairs on his wrists glinting in the blaze.

When they had eaten dessert, which consisted of the promised tin of apricots with some chocolate digestive biscuits Ashley found in a cookie jar, Lucas pushed aside the trolley of empty plates and poured them coffee from a thermos jug. Switching out the light on the end table, so that the room was lit only by the flickering fire, he sat next to her on the sofa, his arm resting along the back. His long fingers played with a strand of her lustrous hair.

Her breath caught in her throat. It was as if her whole being tremulously waited for him to become bolder in his caresses. In an effort to appear in control she picked up her cup of coffee. The spoon rattled in the saucer, her hand shook so hard.

She heard Lucas chuckle softly, then he took her untasted coffee from her, and turning her so that she lay back against the cushions he proceeded to kiss her very slowly and deliberately. His lips brushed her eyelids and gently grazed her cheek. He nibbled on her earlobe until at last his mouth came to rest at the hollow of her throat.

'Sweetheart, you're so lovely . . . I want you so much,' he murmured thickly.

The blood pounded in her body, making speech impossible. Wave after wave of sensation pulsed through her and she was filled with a wild compelling ache in the very core of her being. When Lucas turned and half lay on her she arched her soft body against him, matching his passion with her own. His hard muscled torso crushed hers and she felt his breath quicken. His mouth took possession of hers again, and now his kiss was demanding, urgent. His skilful fingers undid the top buttons of her dress and he stroked her satiny skin, caressing and arousing her until she thought she would faint with desire.

Finally he released his tight hold on her and looked into her flushed face. His eyes were blurred with passion. 'Sweet . . . sweet Ashley,' he said huskily, smoothing back her tangled red curls with trembling hands. 'Let's stay here the night. We can drive to the set together tomorrow morning . . .'

Sanity began to return to Ashley's dazed mind. What was she thinking of? She wasn't thinking—that was the problem. She was appalled at the way she had allowed herself to lead him on. But she was helpless under the expert seduction of his mouth and caresses. Even now her limbs turned to water at the sight of his ardent face. She forced herself into an upright position and buttoned her dress with quivering fingers.

'No, Lucas . . . we . . . we mustn't.'

'Sweetheart . . .' He made to clasp her in his arms again, but she stood up, eluding him, putting distance between them.

'Please, Lucas . . . I don't want to . . .'

'That's a lie, Ashley. You want me just as much as I want you,' he said harshly.

'That . . . that's not the point,' she faltered.

'What is the point, then?' he demanded. 'Why this sudden attack of marmoreal chastity?'

'I'm not keen on joining clubs!' she flashed at him, stung by his sarcasm.

'Joining clubs?' His dark brows arched.

'The Lucas Martineaux Mistress club.' Ashley set her rounded chin defiantly. 'It has enough members already!'

His eyes narrowed to slits. 'Are you judging me?' He asked coldly.

'No. But I do judge myself.' She was regaining her

equanimity and spoke without hesitation. 'I know that a casual affair would make me very unhappy. I want more out of life than a series of short-term love affairs.' She looked at him unwaveringly.

His lips twisted cynically. 'Most actresses wouldn't agree with you.'

'I'm not most actresses,' she replied. 'I think I'd be very stupid to do something I'd regret, simply to conform with your biased view of actresses.'

'I do believe you're on the level!' Lucas shook his head in disbelief and going to the window peered at the night. 'It's clearing.' He turned and smiled wryly. 'You're saved from a fate worse than death. Let's do the dishes, then I'll drive you back to the hotel.'

Later, while Lucas was raking out the ashes of the fire, Ashley tidied herself in the bathroom. She combed out her tangled wealth of hair, then stared intently into the wooden-framed mirror.

'Virtue is its own reward,' she whispered comfortingly to her pale reflection. But remembering her ardent response to Lucas's lovemaking, she ruefully admitted that her behaviour hadn't been particularly virtuous. Which was possibly why, instead of feeling rewarded, she felt miserably thwarted and filled with unsatisfied longing. Loving him and wanting him more than ever.

CHAPTER EIGHT

ON the set the following morning Ashley found it hard to reconcile the memory of yesterday's boyish, passionate Lucas with the stony man who greeted her now. He was withdrawn, and so punctiliously courteous that she was chilled to the bone. He had been like that ever since they had left Hackmatack, and she could only conclude that having suffered rejection at her hands he wanted to punish her. He was behaving quite normally with everyone else on the set, it was only with her he was aloof, and it hurt her more than she cared to admit to be singled out for this unjust treatment.

Thank God I didn't spend the night with him, she reflected, I'd be feeling even worse than I do now. Because there was no denying he had succeeded in making her utterly miserable. She found his coldness harder to bear than his anger. It was monstrous of him to behave to her this way, she fumed, trying, without success, to hate him.

When Sloane arrived Lucas greeted her warmly, kissing her cheek, telling her how beautiful she looked in a handsome buckskin cloak, asking her if she was warm enough.

Clucking over her like a bloody hen! Ashley thought viciously. She caught him looking at her out of the corner of his eye, and willed herself not to betray, by so much as the hint of a blush, the misery he was causing her.

When the camera started rolling she made a monumental effort and emptied her mind of everything except the scene being shot. She remembered all Lucas had told her of cinema technique, and did her best to apply it. Her rigorous drama training stood her in good stead. She had been schooled how to focus her concentration to the exclusion of all personal problems, and she applied this now.

As the morning progressed so did her confidence. At least as far as her work was concerned she was a success. And from the way her private life was going, it looked as if work was going to be her only consolation.

When they broke for lunch Maggy gave her a 'thumbs up' sign and whispered a hasty, 'Nice going, honey!'

At the lodge, where lunch was waiting for them, Ashley made a point of seating herself between Tim, and Jock the sound man. She didn't want to give Lucas the opportunity to snub her. This way she was protected.

He came in after the company was seated and stood at the door, his hair falling over his forehead in disarray. When he saw her next to Tim his grim expression became even grimmer. He didn't make any move to join them, but searching down the length of the table called out imperiously, 'I'm going into the village, Sloane. Want to come and grab a hamburger with me?'

'*Divine*, darling,' Sloane crowed triumphantly, throwing a silk scarf over her raven hair, 'an *assignation*! I couldn't be happier!' She fluttered her lashes at the company in general and at Ashley in particular. 'We may *never* return,' she simpered.

Lucas looked irritated. 'Get a move on, Sloane,' he said ungraciously, 'we've only got an hour.'

Ashley concentrated on her lunch, pushing the boeuf bourguignon around on her plate. That little scene had caused her to lose what little appetite she'd had. When she heard the door slam announcing they had left, she gave up all pretence of eating, and pushed her plate away.

'Now, lassie,' said the fatherly Jock, 'you need to eat more than that. That's not enough to keep a bird alive.'

'I ate too many doughnuts during the morning,' she lied.

'I wouldn't have thought you had the time,' Jock observed, 'you've been on camera nearly all morning.'

Tim broke in. 'And from what I hear you're doing a great job. Congratulations, beautiful!'

'Lucas gave me a drama lesson. It helped,' she told

them. Even mentioning his name was an agony for her.

'He had to have the talent to work with, lassie,' Jock said bluntly.

'I didn't seem to be burdened with talent the other day.' Ashley smiled wryly at the memory of her first, disastrous performance. 'You must have been worried.'

'Of course we weren't worried, beautiful,' Tim said gallantly. 'After all, Luc picked you, and Luc always picks winners.'

'I wish he'd exercise the same taste with his choice of luncheon companions,' the Scotsman growled. 'I thought that old romance was dead and buried.'

'Not if La Sheppard wants to reactivate it.' Tim spoke across Ashley. 'And word is out that she's after him again. She may wind up as Madame Martineaux after all.'

Jock wiped his mouth on his paper napkin. 'Well, that's one wedding I won't dance at,' he said. 'I'd consider it more in the category of a wake.' He turned his attention to Ashley, who, trapped between them, was listening unwillingly to this conversation. 'I canna stand the woman,' he went on, 'she's a phoney. Luc's worth better.'

Even though she could have kissed Jock for his opinion, Ashley had to escape. Sitting here listening to a discussion about Lucas's love-life was more than she could bear. Excusing herself, she pulled on her parka over her costume.

'If you wait a minute, beautiful, I'll come too,' Tim offered.

Smiling, she shook her head. 'Thanks, Tim, but like Garbo, "I vant to be alone",' she said, escaping through the door. She needed some sort of exertion. A brisk walk in the cold might help.

It was a brilliantly sunny day, with a cloudless sky like blue enamel. The brightness dazzled her, making her blink for a moment in the glare. The hard-packed snow squeaked under her feet as she set off down the road.

She noticed that a path had been cleared down the side of the incline to Devil's River, to enable the camera crew to take shots of the sunset later on. She decided to go down to take a closer look at the water. The descent was easy, for this part of the hill was not thickly wooded, and the track was wide.

She reached the river bank without any difficulty, and stood looking at the unfrozen centre of the rapids, where deep water, the colour of gunpowder, twisted and foamed against the river's ice-clogged sides. The turbulence of the stream seemed to match her own mood. It had a hypnotic effect. She wanted to get a closer look at this roaring water harnessed between thick sheets of ice.

Cautiously she stepped off the snowy bank and felt her way across the frozen edge of the river. It felt quite solid. The wind had blown the snow away, and the ice looked like pewter under her feet. She looked down into the green-black depths. Under the thick crust the current darted, like tongues of silver flame. The rushing, leaping water, rang in her ears, fascinating and frightening her. It was as if the river was alive—malignant, threatening, but so beautiful she was mesmerised and incapable of moving back to the safe bank.

Then, with terrifying rapidity, several things happened simultaneously. There was a series of loud cracks, like pistol shots. The ice starred beneath her feet, and the piece on which she was standing broke away and tilted, so that she fell heavily, with her legs in the freezing river. She managed to keep her body out of the water by pulling herself up on the broken slab of ice, but she was soaked to her knees, and the ice was tilting dangerously. The bitter cold water clawed and tugged at her long skirt like a ravening animal. She clung desperately to the slippery ice. She heard Lucas's voice shouting her name, then out of the corner of her eye she caught sight of him hurling himself full length on the ice, in order to reach her.

'Hang on, Ashley!' he shouted as he slid himself, inch by inch, towards her.

The cold was so intense it felt like a knife slashing at her. Then Lucas grasped her under her armpits. Slowly he pulled her over the listing ice, which creaked

ominously with their combined weight, until he had
manoeuvred them back to the safety of the shore.

He tore off his parka and wrapped it around her legs,
gently chafing her calves to restore her circulation. She
started to cry with relief and shock.

'There, there, love . . . it's OK, you're safe now,' he
crooned, and tucking the parka snugly around her he
lifted her up in his powerful arms and carried her up the
hill, back to the Lodge.

Ashley's panic started to recede and she was over-
whelmingly conscious of the joy of being in his arms, her
head resting on his shoulder. It didn't matter that he'd
been remote and cruel to her all morning, or that he was
having an affair with Sloane and simply flirted with other
women to pass the time. All that mattered at this
moment was the reality of his strong arms and comforting presence. Her tears dried on her cheeks, and with a
sigh she gave herself up to this fleeting heaven.

After they arrived at the Lodge events became
blurred. People milled around asking questions. She
caught sight of Tim, his face shocked, and heard
Sloane's querulous voice asking what was going on.

Lucas ignored them all and carried her into the make-
up winnebago, where he laid her down gently.

'Get Wardrobe to change her into her own clothes,' he
said to Maggy, who had followed them in, 'and phone
for a doctor to be at the hotel. I'll drive her back in the
station wagon myself. We'll wrap for today. See to it,
will you, Maggy?'

Ashley tried to say that she'd be all right to work, once
she'd changed out of her wet boots and stockings, but
the words wouldn't come out, and her feet and legs were
now tingling so painfully she doubted she could stand.
So she lay back on the padded seat and let the dresser
peel off her wet things. She was bundled into her snow-
suit, and wrapped up in a warm blanket. Lucas came
back and lifted her up in his arms again and carried her to
the waiting car that was warmed up and ready to go. He
lay her on the back seat, tucking the blanket round
her.

'Lucas, I . . . I'll be all right . . . I don't . . .' she quavered.

'Sh, Red.' His voice and hands were gentle. 'Don't fret, everything's OK.'

He climbed into the driver's seat and switched on the radio, twisting the dial until he found some soft music.

'There you are, Red.' He turned to look back at her, lying on the seat, small in her cocoon of blankets. 'Listen to the music, honey . . . take your mind off things.'

Ashley drifted between sleep and waking during the drive back. But every time she closed her eyes she felt again the ice slipping beneath her, and the sound of the car's engine, under the radio, turned into the roar of the wild grey water. So she struggled to keep her eyes open by staring at the back of Lucas's dark curly head.

The doctor was waiting for them at the hotel. He was a kindly French Canadian, around sixty. He looked grave indeed when he heard what had happened.

'The Devil's River! At this time of year . . . *mon Dieu!*'

Lucas carried her to her chalet, then left her with the doctor.

'You are very lucky, *mademoiselle*,' he said at the end of his examination, 'there is no frostbite. You were not long enough in the water to do damage.'

'That's because of Lucas . . . he saved me . . .' To her dismay Ashley started to cry again. 'Oh dear, I don't know why I'm . . .'

'*Naturellement!* It is the shock. Now change into your night things and get into bed. I will prescribe a sedative to calm your nerves. In the morning all will be forgotten. You will be yourself again. Now I will leave you and reassure your young man who is so anxious.'

'He . . . he's not my . . .' Ashley started to correct him, but he had already bustled out of the chalet.

She undressed and put on a cream flannel nightgown, ruffled and Victorian. She felt as weak as a kitten.

When she had crawled under the covers Lucas came back, with a glass of warm milk on a tray. His briefcase was under his arm.

'Here you are, Red—doctor's orders. You're to drink this and take this pill.' He held out a paper cup with a large white pill in it.

Obediently she did as she was told, handing the empty glass back to him. Her grey eyes were like two shadowed pools in her ashen face.

'Lucas, I'm . . . I'm so sorry,' she whispered, blinking away the tears of weakness that came unbidden.

'Forget it, Ashley,' he commanded. 'It was an accident, don't worry about it.'

'At least let me say thank you . . . for saving me,' she gulped.

Lucas gave her a lopsided smile. 'Think nothing of it. Rescuing damsels in distress is a sideline of mine,' she tried to say something, 'and knocking them unconscious when they refuse to go to sleep is another. So *shut up* and close your eyes,' he laid the tips of his fingers on her well-defined eyelids. 'Are you warm enough?' Eyes tight shut, she nodded. 'Good! I'll stay here till you're asleep.'

She heard him settle himself in one of the easy chairs. His briefcase clicked open and papers rustled. The pill started to work and she drifted into sleep, pretending Lucas still had his arms about her.

They were skimming down a tree-lined slope on a giant toboggan. Down, down they sped, towards the icy turbulent river. She tried to warn him, but no sound came, and turning, she was horrified to discover that it wasn't Lucas sitting behind her on the speeding toboggan, but Sloane, her black hair fluttering Medusa-like, her eyes burning with hate. The ice yawned open to receive them, and Sloane pushed Ashley down into the raging water, which closed over her head, suffocating her, dragging and clawing. She tried to scream for Lucas, but the bitter cold water clogged her scream in her throat . . .

'Sweetheart, it's OK . . . Ashley honey, it's all right . . .' He was sitting on the bed holding her in his arms. But this wasn't a dream; it was reality. He was there with her, warm and comforting. She gave a sob and put her arms round his waist, burrowing her head into his chest.

'Oh, Lucas! The water . . . the water . . .' she gasped. She pressed her cheek against the crisp black hair at the vee of his shirt.

'Sh, baby! It was only a dream. You're safe now.' Gently he disengaged himself from her encircling arms and pushed her back on the pillows.

She noticed that the sun was setting and the room was filled with purplish-pink light. 'Oh, Lucas—your sunset! The last shot of the day. I've made you miss it!'

'Don't worry about it, honey. Steve's out shooting it now. They don't need me for that.' He put his hand up to her forehead and stroked back a wandering strand of coppery hair. His dark eyes were filled with such warmth that she couldn't trust herself to look into them, for fear she would burst into tears again, and throw herself into his arms.

'How did you happen to be there when the . . . the ice gave way?' She still shuddered at the memory of those pistol-like cracks.

'I'd come back early. I wanted . . . to talk to you. Then I saw you from the road.' His face became solemn. 'You scared the living daylights out of me. That was a really dumb thing to do, Red. You could have drowned!'

'I . . . I know. I'm sorry.'

Lucas got up and went for his coat. 'Well, it's over now. You were lucky. If I hadn't been there . . .' he paused, his coat half on, 'you're not the only one who's going to have nightmares for a while.'

She fiddled with the sheet. There was nothing she could say.

He finished putting on his coat. 'Particularly since after this morning's work you'd be impossible to re-place.'

She stopped fiddling and looked up at him. So *that* was his principal concern! The problem of finding her re-placement. Her cheeks grew pink for the first time since her accident.

'I'm sure you would have managed, Lucas,' she said,

her voice gaining strength with indignation. 'From the way you ignored me all morning I didn't think you'd noticed I was on the set at all!'

What am I *saying*? she thought wildly. It must be that pill I've taken. It's removed my inhibitions.

He had opened the door and stood silhouetted against the fiery sky. 'Did you think that? Did you *really* think that? My God, Ashley, if only that was true!' He slammed the door shut and rapidly crossed the room to her bed. His face was white under his tan. 'You're driving me *mad*!' he rasped. 'I can't sleep, I can't work. I've never felt like this—never!'

Ashley stared up at him, her eyes wide as saucers.

'And you're such an innocent,' he went on. 'At first I thought it was all an act . . . that virginal quality of yours. But after a while I realised it was for real . . . that you're not just a clever little actress putting on an act . . . you really are like that. And then I was . . . *scared*.' He pushed his long fingers through his thick black curls, making them wilder than ever.

'Scared? What were you scared of?'

He took a deep breath. His face was grave. 'Of being so crazy in love with you.' His voice broke. 'Don't you understand? I'm telling you that I love you.'

Her heart beat suddenly—joyfully—then she remembered. 'But . . . what about Sloane?'

'What about her?' Lucas seemed genuinely mystified. 'That was over years ago.'

'But this morning . . . you seemed so . . . attentive.'

'I was trying to hurt you,' he admitted harshly. 'I thought, if you didn't want me, then I'd show you that I *didn't* care.' He gave a hollow laugh. 'The only thing wrong with that scheme was that I *did*.' He looked down at her bleakly. 'Knowing the power you exert over me should give you a good laugh,' he said with bitterness as he turned to leave.

'Lucas!' She leapt out of bed and ran to him on shaky legs, taking his arm to prevent him leaving. In her long flannel nightgown she looked like a child. Her russet head didn't quite reach his shoulder. 'Lucas, stop! I had no idea . . . I mean . . . Oh, darling Lucas, it's wonderful . . . because I feel the same!'

He stood motionless, looking into her clear, shining eyes. 'You mean . . . ?'

She nodded up at him, her titian hair tumbling over her shoulders. 'I love you too, darling . . . but I thought . . . you and Sloane . . .'

He gave an inarticulate cry and gathered her into his arms, covering her face with kisses, finally pressing his lips on her eager ones. When he at last raised his mouth from hers, he pushed both hands into her heavy scented hair, and tilted her head back in order to scrutinise her face.

'You're like a silver bowl filled to the brim with sweet water,' he said softly. 'Clean and innocent.' He lifted her in his arms. 'And you'll catch your death of cold standing around in your bare feet like this.' Gently he deposited her back on the bed and sat beside her, stroking her face and twining a tendril of her silky hair in his fingers.

Ashley felt a fluttering in the pit of her stomach. His physical closeness, the warm scent of him, filled her with wild yearnings. She thrust her hands inside his open overcoat. She could feel the warmth of his flesh through his shirt. His heart was thudding like a wild animal's.

'Why don't you take off your coat, Lucas?' she said huskily.

He did as she suggested, dropping it on the floor, then he lay beside her, pressing the length of his hard body against hers. He kissed her again, the pressure of his lips parting hers. At the touch of his mouth Ashley felt such a stab of desire that she moaned with pleasure and gave herself up mindlessly to sensation. The world now consisted of Lucas and herself—their bodies fused together. Nothing else existed. Nothing else mattered. She had never dreamt she could feel like this—so reckless, so ardent. He stroked her expertly, feeding her passion. When he unbuttoned the bodice of her nightgown she arched herself, so that he could kiss her perfect rosy breast, driving them both to further heights of burning need.

'Yes . . . yes . . .' she murmured brokenly, sliding her hands inside his shirt, caressing his naked chest. His breath grew ragged with urgent desire. He drew away from her in order to remove his shirt, and looked down on her as she lay back on the pillow, naked to the waist, her face flushed, her eyes trusting.

He gave a deep shuddering sigh, and getting up from the bed gently drew the sheet up to cover her to her chin.

'No, Red . . . not like this,' he said with finality.

A blush of humiliation swept over her, from her toes to the crown of her head. She clutched the sheet tightly. 'Did I . . . did I do something wrong?' she asked, her voice small with shame.

'No, my sweetheart. No.' He made a step towards her, then stopped himself. 'You're generous and loving . . . all innocent passion,' his face glowed with love, 'but I want this . . . us . . . to be different. I don't want just another location affair with you, Ashley. There've been too many of those in my life.'

'I don't want to know about them,' she said quickly.

'You mustn't have any illusions about me Ashley. There have been many women in my life . . . I'm not proud of it . . . but what I feel for you is quite, quite different.'

'I . . . I see,' she said. But she was shattered by his sudden rejection.

'I'm not sure you do, my darling. I'm not sure I understand myself. But I want to . . . to *court* you, Red, to give you time to get to know me. I want you to meet my family . . .' he gave her a crooked smile, 'old-fashioned stuff like that.'

Her heart rose, a bird winging.

'Let's finish this picture, and when it's over . . .'

Her heart stopped its flight. 'I fly back to England,' she said miserably.

'And I'll join you there before I start rehearsals in New York. I can meet your folks and we can discuss our future then.'

Ashley gave a little gasp of happiness. 'I don't have many folks,' she said, 'just my mother and my aunt.'

'Then I'll meet your mother and your aunt. Does that sound like a reasonable arrangement?' She nodded her head on the pillow and gave him a tremulous smile. 'And don't imagine for one minute that it's easy for me not to make love to you right now, Ashley. I want you and love you more than you can guess. That's what I was going to tell you when you so dramatically fell into the river.'

'You were?' Happiness was washing over her in waves.

'Yes, honey. I'd decided I couldn't fight it any more. It doesn't matter that you're an actress, or extravagant as the devil . . .'

'Oh, Lucas, I'm not—really! It's not what you think . . .' she tried to explain, but he silenced her.

'We won't discuss it, sweetheart, because it doesn't matter any more. I *accept* you just the way you are. And now,' he picked up his coat, 'I'm going to leave you to get some rest. I've got work to do. And you've had quite a day.' He kissed her chastely on the forehead, then traced the line of her cheek with his thumb. 'Sleep well, my lovely wanton. Dream of me,' he whispered, 'and remember that I love you.'

Ashley lay in the darkness hugging her happiness to her like a blanket. A future with Lucas! It was more than she had dared to dream of.

She was glad now that he had not possessed her when she had offered herself so impetuously—her cheeks burned at the memory—like him, she wanted more than a furtive liaison.

Sleepily she fastened the buttons on her nightgown. Recalling his lips on her breast, she felt a faint stirring of desire deep inside her, like the concentric ripples on a pool, or the muffled echo of a distant bell.

CHAPTER NINE

As the doctor had promised, the following morning Ashley felt fine. However, her mental state was somewhat chaotic. That wonderful time with Lucas yesterday evening seemed like a dream, and she wondered fearfully if he had changed his mind since then and was perhaps regretting his fervent declaration of love.

She needn't have worried. When her driver tapped on her door at six a.m. he handed her a single yellow chrysanthemum and a page torn from a notebook. In the car she unfolded the paper and read, in Lucas's strong masculine hand, 'Good morning, my darling. The florists aren't open at five a.m., so you'll have to make do with a flower stolen from the hotel lobby. I would like to buy you a glade of gardenias, this flower is just a stand-in. I love you. Lucas.'

Vibrant with joy, she carefully folded the note and put it in her purse. She smelt the aromatic scent of the chrysanthemum blossom and tucked it behind her ear, where it looked like a miniature sun threaded through her chestnut hair. She was so happy that she had to speak or burst.

'Isn't it a *marvellous* morning?' She almost sang to her somnolent driver.

Startled, he nodded. 'Huh! I guess so. Ask me in a couple of hours, when I've come to.'

Ashley gave him a smile of such radiance it was like sunshine in the car. 'It's going to be a lovely day,' she bubbled, 'just *lovely*!' I must stop babbling or people will think I'm insane, she silently cautioned herself. But her childlike mouth was still curved in a smile of sheer bliss when they drove into the Tremblant Lodge parking lot, and it was still there while Jane made her up.

'You're looking very chipper this morning, Ashley,' Jane remarked, smoothing shadow just below the delicate sweep of Ashley's brows. 'Falling in the river seems to have agreed with you.'

Ashley chuckled deep in her throat. 'It's like hitting your head with a hammer—it's great when you stop!'

'Well, you're certainly blooming.' Jane looked at her critically. 'Thank goodness you don't have to look wan and wasted for today's scenes. I'd have my work cut out!'

After her make-up and hair were completed Ashley went into the Lodge to get a cup of coffee before the morning's work started. As she pushed open the heavy door her heart started hammering painfully. Would Lucas be there? She was longing to see him again—and terrified—and generally feeling as if she was walking on a delicious tightrope.

He was standing by the coffee machine talking to Maggy, but most of his attention was focused on the entrance, and the moment Ashley was in sight he excused himself and crossed over to her.

As he approached her she realised that he was feeling as nervous as she was. His eyes were shadowed with anxiety. He smiled at her tentatively—Lucas tentative?—her heart went out to him. Before he could say a word she reached out and took his hand.

'Thank you for my lovely flower, Luc darling. It was the loveliest "good morning" I've ever had.' She indicated the chrysanthemum that she now wore pulled through the zipper-tab of her parka.

'I . . . I'm glad you liked it,' he said. He seemed uncharacteristically tongue-tied, but the anxiety had gone out of his eyes. He leaned forward, and in full view of Maggy and the crew he lightly kissed her lips. 'Do you feel better this morning?'

'I feel *wonderful* this morning!' She gazed up at him, radiant.

Lucas gave a soft laugh and squeezed her hand. 'I can see that. Being in love agrees with you.'

'Mmm,' she nodded her head vigorously, 'it also makes me very hungry. Is there any food left?'

He went with her to the laden breakfast table where Maggy and several crew members were tactfully watching them. 'I forgot you didn't get dinner last night,' he said. 'Then you must eat a good breakfast now, Red. Understood?'

This was more like the old Lucas—the bossy one! But she no longer resented this. It showed he loved her, was concerned about her. She poured herself hot coffee and bit her even white teeth into a bagel smothered in cream cheese and marmalade.

While Lucas discussed the first shot of the day with Maggy, he kept an arm around Ashley's shoulders. This seemingly casual possessiveness filled her with such happiness she felt as if at any moment her feet would leave the ground and she would fly. Showing his affection so openly surely proved that he loved her in a special way, that what was between them was more than a casual, furtive affair.

Sloane arrived and characteristically posed in the doorway for a moment before entering, scanning the room with large dark eyes, which narrowed to slits when she noticed Lucas's proprietorial arm round Ashley. She glided towards them, and Ashley's heart began to flutter nervously in her breast. But Lucas didn't remove his arm.

'Morning, Sloane,' he said affably. 'Have some coffee?'

Sloane ignored this. 'You're recovered, are you?' she said to Ashley, her mouth twisting with dislike.

Ashley met her look unwaveringly. 'Yes, thank you.'

'I wondered,' Sloane persisted, 'since Lucas appears to be holding you up.'

Lucas gave a snort of laughter. 'If I wasn't in such a good mood this morning, Sloane, I might ask what business it is of yours. But I'm too happy to start an argument.' He turned to Ashley. 'If you're ready, honey, I'll drive you in the jeep.' She nodded, uncomfortably aware of Sloane's eyes burning with malice, but his arm was still around her shoulders when they left the Lodge.

In the jeep she broached the subject. 'I'm afraid Sloane's upset, Lucas.'

He waved aside her fears. 'She has no reason to be upset. I told you, it's been over between us for years. And she has to learn about us sooner or later. Don't worry, honey, she can't hurt us.' Ashley took his advice. In any case, she was far too happy to brood.

The morning sped by. She discovered, to her delight, that the rapport between them extended to their work. She could sense what Lucas wanted from her in a scene almost without words. The emotional security she felt with him gave her more confidence in her performance. She blossomed, both as a woman and as an actress, under the warmth of his love.

By the end of the day everyone was aware that Lucas and Ashley were romantically involved—and everyone seemed to be delighted. Even dour Jock smiled on them like a benign Scottish Father Christmas. There were only two exceptions to the general bonhomie—Sloane and Tim. Ashley bumped into Tim on her way back to her chalet that evening, and he regarded her balefully.

'Am I supposed to congratulate you?' he asked.

She answered him coolly. 'I don't understand you, Tim. Congratulate me for what?'

'For landing Lucas. Everyone says you're a couple now.'

Ashley's delicate nostrils flared. 'I don't like your tone, Tim. As for Lucas and me being a "couple", as you put it . . . we love each other, if that's what you mean.'

The fight seemed to drain out of Tim. He looked comically woebegone. 'Sorry, beautiful, didn't mean to be rude, only . . . heck, it's hard losing you to the boss! Even if the boss is a great guy.'

'You can't lose what you've never had, Tim,' she pointed out.

He nodded regretfully. 'I guess that's true. But you can't blame a guy for trying, Ashley.'

She took his arm and squeezed it. 'Dear Tim! You're very flattering. I'm touched—really.'

'You also look happy, Ashley.' He leant forward and gave her a brotherly kiss on her soft cheek. 'He's a lucky man.'

And Lucas behaved like one! That evening when they ate at the company table he glowed with pride. Ashley, sitting beside him, her hair burnished by the lamplight, her face bright above the polo neck of her yellow sweater, felt as if she was in heaven.

Later Lucas took her to a local bar. 'We'll only stay for an hour, Red,' he told her, 'I have to look at the daily rushes, and you must get your rest. But we can dance here and I must hold you in my arms for a while . . . I don't trust myself to do that back at the hotel.' He brushed his lips across her forehead and murmured, 'I'm like an open can of gasoline and you're a match.'

'How romantic, darling!' she giggled. 'You make us sound like a garage!' But she knew what he meant, for when he held her on the dance floor her legs threatened to give way under her, she trembled so much.

They danced without speaking for nearly an hour. He leaned his cheek against the side of her silky head and held her close. She shut her eyes and gloried in the feel of his strong arms around her, his breath warm against her delicate ear, his hard thighs thrusting against hers. When they left, the coffee and brandy they had ordered remained untasted on the table. And when he kissed her goodnight outside her chalet and then quickly turned and left her, she knew it was because neither of them could have resisted the demand of their desire if he had lingered.

The days that followed were some of the happiest in Ashley's life. Not that she and Lucas had much time to spend alone together. There were sometimes night scenes to be shot, and the morning call was always early. She learned to catnap on the set at odd times, or to curl up in the back of a car or the make-up winnebago when she wasn't needed, and catch up on her sleep that way.

Most evenings Lucas had meetings with his cameraman, or with Maggy, or the producers of the film. He had to view the daily rushes, which took time. On their one free day he had to work on his upcoming stage production of *King Lear*, and Ashley had lines to learn for the following week's shoot. On those days they would sit on either side of the hotel fireplace, Lucas with his Shakespeare text and notebook, Ashley curled up with her script. The logs would crackle, and every once in a while their eyes would meet. He would smile at her, his black eyes smouldering, and a surge of pure joy would spread over her. Later they would walk to the village and eat at one of the elegant restaurants there. Then they would walk back again through the frosty night, exchanging stories about their childhood, or discussing their views of the play he would be doing in New York.

'It's rather a monastic life at the moment, my sweetheart,' Lucas apologised, 'but it has to be that way while I'm working. Not much fun for you.'

'I'm not complaining, darling. I've never been happier,' Ashley assured him. This was true. Even Sloane had ceased to trouble her. That sultry beauty was spending more and more free time with her friends at L'Esterel, and the rumour was that a wealthy business man was now the focus of her attention. She had reverted to being condescendingly polite, which suited Ashley very well. She was grateful that this problem seemed to have resolved itself.

During this time she didn't mention anything about sending all her money home to her family. Nor did she tell Lucas that the reason she was so well dressed had nothing to do with extravagance, but was because of her aunt's gift for making clothes. The truth was, she hardly ever thought to tell him, and the few times she did he was usually involved with either some technicality about the film or the play, and the timing seemed wrong. She decided to tell him all about her reasons for needing money so desperately when the film was finished and they had the traditional 'wrap party'. There was no pressing need to bother him now.

On one of their free days Lucas decided not to work, but to take her to meet his family. She was happy about this, but nevertheless very nervous at the prospect, and she dressed with special care. They were to spend the afternoon and evening with Lucas's father in his Montreal home. She prayed her cream wool suit, teamed with a kingfisher-blue silk blouse, would be acceptable. Aunt Connie had fashioned the blouse with a high collar and deep cuffs trimmed with narrow ruffles of the same material. Ashley piled her hair high in a topknot of gleaming curls, and sprayed herself with l'Air du Temps perfume from a huge bottle Lucas had given her as a surprise present the day before. She wouldn't wear her toque today, she decided. She'd chance freezing her ears for the sake of making a good impression on the Martineaux clan.

Monsieur Martineaux's house was situated on a broad tree-lined avenue in the French suburb of Outremont. It had been snowing earlier, but now the sun had come out, and the snow-ploughs were busy clearing the streets, piling the sparkling fresh snow into silvery heaps on either side of the road. The driveway to the large bow-windowed house was clear, and already a red sedan car stood near the front door, which was unlatched ready for Lucas's arrival.

They entered the spacious tiled hall and removed their coats and boots. At that moment the drawing room door opened and two small cannonballs hurled themselves at Lucas, squealing and shrieking in a high-pitched mixture of French and English. Laughing, Lucas squatted down and hugged the two children, a boy and a little girl, in his arms.

'Steady, *mes enfants*,' he exclaimed. He rose and turned to Ashley, who was standing in a corner. 'Red, these two toughs are Roger and Andrea, my niece and nephew. Children, meet Ashley Morrison. Ashley is *une comédienne* in my film.' Two pairs of ruthless blue eyes bored into Ashley. 'Where are your manners, Roger?' Lucas gave the brown-haired little boy a push towards her. 'Say hello.'

'*Bonjour, mademoiselle*,' the small boy piped.

'*En anglais*, Roger,' Lucas prompted.

Ashley held her hand out to the child, who took it shyly. '*Bonjour*, Roger. Won't you call me Ashley? All my friends do.' Roger did not commit himself, but continued to stare. She turned to his sister who was clinging to Lucas's hand. 'Hello, Andrea . . . what a pretty name that is!' Andrea put the end of one of her dark blonde braids in her mouth and buried her head in her uncle's leg.

'They're a bit overcome at the moment,' Lucas grinned. 'Give them time.' He turned his attention back to the children. 'Now, you two! Where is Grandpère?'

'*Dans le salon*—in the drawing room,' they chanted in a bilingual chorus, dragging their uncle towards the double doors at the end of the hall. Lucas extricated himself from the childish hands pulling at him and put his arm around Ashley.

'Ready to meet the Martineaux family, Red?' he smiled. 'Or are you regretting the whole thing?'

'Of course I'm not,' she said stoutly. But she was feeling very selfconscious nevertheless.

She soon discovered her fears were groundless. Monsieur Martineaux did his best to make her welcome and so did the other members of the family. She was settled in a wing-chair near the blazing log fire and given sherry in an antique cut-crystal glass. Sitting back sipping her drink, she had time to observe the room and its occupants.

Lucas's father was younger looking than his photograph. But that was partly due, she thought, to the fact that his silver hair, which was as unruly as his eldest son's, must have been smoothed by the hairbrush for the picture. This gave him a sleeker, older look.

His only daughter, Marie-André, calmed her two excited children. She was an attractive, brown-haired woman, rounded without being plump, dressed with exquisite French chic. Her husband, Glen, a quiet smiling man of English extraction, completed the party.

Ashley sat back, her skirt fanned out against the darkness of the velvet chair like a pigeon's wing. She liked this spacious panelled room, and particularly admired the attractive paintings and some excellent examples of early Eskimo sculpture exhibited casually on various tables.

Marie-André chatted vivaciously about England, which she knew well through her husband's family, and Monsieur Martineaux, who was knowledgeable about many historic buildings in Britain, joined in energetically. By the time luncheon was announced Ashley felt quite at ease with this lively, bi-cultural group.

She was formally introduced to Marthe, the resident housekeeper, who had been with the Martineaux's for many years. After Ashley had shaken hands with that formidable lady, who had no intention of accepting her at first glance, they all trooped into the dining room.

It was a formal meal, since Marthe had the rest of the day free and had planned to visit friends. They ate rack of lamb which melted in the mouth, potatoes mashed with cream, and French beans sliced thin and served with toasted almonds. The gravy was clear and flavoured with cognac in the French style. After the dessert had been dealt with, an immense flan concocted of pears and nuts, Marthe brought in a silver coffee tray which she deposited in front of Marie-André. She then departed for her friends' amid elaborate instructions about the evening supper which Ashley and Lucas would share with his father and Philippe, the youngest son.

They sat around the dining room table for their coffee in the European fashion. The children were excused to go and play, but they were still fascinated by this stranger in their midst and hung around their mother's chair staring at Ashley with relentless curiosity.

'Are you Uncle Luc's girl-friend?' Andrea's piercing voice cut through the hum of adult conversation.

Lucas gently pulled one of her braids. 'She certainly is.'

'Can you make angels in the snow?' Roger asked her. This was a clear challenge.

'I don't know. I've never tried.' Ashley smiled into the child's serious face. 'Could you teach me?'

'I 'spect so. It's not hard to do,' he said with withering eight-year-old disdain.

'Ah no, Roger!' his mother broke in. 'Poor Ashley's pretty skirt would get wet.'

'It dries fast,' said Ashley, finishing her coffee and getting to her feet. 'Come along, Roger, give me a lesson in angel-making.'

'Me too . . . me too!' his sister shrilled. 'I make the *best* angels!'

The children milled around, putting on snow-suits and boots, losing mitts, and generally slowing down the process of getting ready to go out. Lucas offered to drive the party to the top of the Westmount mountain, since there was lots of snow there, and a view for Ashley to admire.

Marie-André finished zipping up her offspring. 'Are you sure about this, Ashley?' she asked, looking fondly at the squirming children. 'These little monsters can be quite tiring.'

'Don't discourage them, love,' Glen butted in, 'we can have a nice quiet afternoon by ourselves.' He grinned at Ashley. 'I'll make you tea when you return to speed your recovery.'

They drove the short distance up to the summit with the children chattering non-stop.

'Why is your hair that colour?' asked Andrea.

'Are you a *famous* actress?' Roger wanted to know. She told him she wasn't.

Andrea's piping little voice rang out next. 'Are you going to marry Uncle Luc?' she asked. Ashley turned bright pink.

'Now that's *enough*, you two,' Lucas butted in. 'Poor Ashley! It's like the Inquisition!'

'If you did marry Uncle Luc you'd be our aunt,' Roger volunteered. 'Would you like that?'

'Why don't we find out if I can learn to make decent snow angels first?' Ashley countered, grateful that they appeared to have arrived at their destination.

They clambered out of the car and she barely had time to admire the view of Montreal spread below the mountain like a carpet girdled by the semi-frozen St Lawrence River, before the children dragged her up into the park to find a snowdrift.

She learned that to make angels you had to fall

backwards into a drift, then wave your arms slowly to create wings in the snow. She became quite good at it, but they decided Lucas's angels were by far the most impressive.

'They're so big,' said Roger with admiration.

'Like the Angel Gabriel,' agreed his uncle smugly.

'Or Lucifer,' teased Ashley.

Above the children's heads he kissed her lightly on the tip of her nose. 'Only good angels around you, sweetheart,' he said.

When making angels palled they had a strenuous snow-fight. They couldn't make snowballs with the powdery snow, it simply refused to cake, so they flung handfuls of the sugary flakes at each other, screaming with laughter, until they were frosted all over and breathless.

They arrived back at the house dishevelled, pink-cheeked, and exhausted.

Glen took charge of the children before going to make the promised cup of tea, and Ashley went up to one of the bathrooms to dry her hair and generally tidy up. Marie-André came up too, and perched herself on the edge of the large marble tub while Ashley towelled her riotous red hair.

'I must say you are a wonderful surprise,' Marie-André commented.

'Surprise? How?' Ashley asked, towelling vigorously.

Marie-André raised a soignée eyebrow. 'Well, Luc has brought some of his girl-friends to visit us, but they were all very . . . very *ordinaire*. None of them have been a bit like you.' She examined the toe of her elegantly shod foot. 'I hope you won't take offence if I say that you don't seem like an actress at all.'

'You don't like actresses?' asked Ashley, wondering if this was a family failing.

'Well, I'm probably being unfair,' Lucas's sister confided. 'The only actress I've really spent time with was Sloane Sheppard, and frankly she was a royal pain.'

'Oh!' Ashley tried to sound noncommittal.

'And Luc says you're a very good actress too. It's just

. . . you're so natural, playing like that with the children. You fit in so well.'

'It's easy to fit in here,' Ashley replied, through a mouthful of hairpins, 'you all make me feel so at home.' She started re-pinning her hair.

Marie-André uncoiled herself from the edge of the bath and standing next to Ashley applied lipstick to her full mouth. 'Well, I just want you to know that I'm very happy for Luc that he's found a girl like you,' she said warmly. She blotted her lips with a tissue. 'He'd kill me if he could hear me say this, but, in spite of his playboy image, he's been very lonely. He needs stability in his life, and even though I can see you're very young, I feel you have that quality.' She stood back to examine her make-up. '*Bon!* Now, if you're ready, shall we go and drink that cup of tea?'

After tea, when the lamps were lit and Marie-André and her husband had left, dragging their unwilling children who had extracted promises from Ashley that she would visit them again as soon as she could, Lucas excused himself and went to the study to do some work.

Monsieur Martineaux indicated the chair opposite his. 'Come, my dear, let us have an apéritif together before supper. I've scarcely talked to you since you arrived.' He crossed to a cabinet containing an assortment of bottles. 'What can I offer you? Some sherry? Campari soda? . . .'

'Campari soda, please,' Ashley said shyly; she was feeling rather selfconscious again, now that she was alone with the patriarch of the family.

'You have made a conquest of my grandchildren,' said Lucas's father, pouring her drink and a sherry for himself. 'It is obvious they adore you.'

She accepted the proffered glass of Campari. 'They're delightful children.'

'I think so. But I am prejudiced, of course.' He raised his glass of straw-pale sherry. '*A votre santé*, Ashley. Welcome to my house.'

'Thank you . . . er . . . *merci*,' she said, her delicate face pink with pleasure.

He chuckled. He had Lucas's deep laugh, but his speech, unlike his children's, was slightly accented. 'And you, Ashley,' he said, settling himself in his chair, 'do you come from a large family?' His eyes, black like his eldest son's, were kind, and she found herself at ease again. She told him of her father's death, and touched lightly on her mother's illness. She didn't mention about their financial straits, for as long as she could get work their money problems were soluble. In any case this, she felt, was of no interest.

When she had finished Monsieur Martineaux reached across and patted her hand paternally. 'Ah, *ma pauvre enfant*. It has been difficult for you sometimes, I think.' He picked up a silver-framed photograph of a smiling, middle-aged woman, her smooth blonde hair touched with grey. 'This is my dearest wife, taken a year before she died.' He made no attempt to diguise his sadness. 'The gap that is left in such circumstances . . . it is hard for all the family . . . particularly the children.' His sympathy touched a chord in her and she lowered her eyes so that he wouldn't see the sudden glitter of tears. 'However, adversity no doubt has helped to make you a sensitive actress—my son tells me you have remarkable talent,' he said when she looked surprised, 'and having met you I see you also have remarkable beauty.'

'Oh, thank you! I . . .' Ashley stuttered, unused to such Gallic adulation.

'Not at all. *C'est vrai.*' He greeted Lucas, who came in at that moment. 'I have been embarrassing this lovely child with my compliments, Lucas. And how I want to give her a present,' he turned back to Ashley.

'A . . . present?' she queried. 'But why?'

'Because I like you. And because you are *charmant*,' he said. 'You will permit me?'

'Of course. Thank you, Monsieur Martineaux.' The dimple at the corner of her mouth deepened. 'It feels like Christmas,' she observed to Lucas, who was obviously pleased that the two of them were getting along so well.

Monsieur Martineaux went to a mahogany desk on

the far side of the room and took a small velvet box out of one of the drawers. 'This I think will suit you,' he said as he handed it to her.

She opened the lid and lifted out a bracelet of elliptical green stones the colour of moss. Each stone was joined to its partner by a gold link. The gems were translucent and smooth with age, as fragile as stained glass. Ashley turned to face Lucas's father, almost speechless with pleasure.

'Oh, they're lovely! I . . .' She jumped up and kissed him on the cheek, then held the delicate piece of jewellery up to the light. 'I've never had such a lovely bracelet . . . I don't know how to thank you . . .'

'They are peridots, from the Edwardian era,' Monsieur Martineaux explained. He was clearly gratified by her delighted reaction. 'I hope you will wear them with pleasure, my dear.'

Lucas fastened it around her slender wrist. 'There you are, Red.' He examined the peridots closely. 'They're the colour your eyes go when you're mad. A very appropriate gift, Papa!' He lightly kissed the inside of her wrist before letting go of her hand. 'And now if you'll excuse us, Ashley can help me prepare supper before you succeed in stealing her away from me.'

In the kitchen Lucas took her in his arms and kissed her hard on the mouth. When the kiss was over he buried his face in her topknot of curls. 'You're an instant hit in this family, Red,' he whispered in her ear, 'a real smasheroo, as we say in this business.'

'I think they're pretty smasheroo themselves,' she answered, her voice husky with happiness. Life had become so enchanted she was lulled by the thought that nothing could go wrong ever again.

Lucas's younger brother Philippe, still dressed in his ski clothes, joined them for their modest evening meal of cold ham and salad, followed by fresh fruit and a ripe Brie cheese. He was quite unlike Lucas in looks, favouring their mother's side of the family. Twenty-four years old and less French in manner than either his father or brother, he was slightly reserved to begin with, but by the end of the meal he and Ashley were enjoying a furious discussion about the pros and cons of theatrical behaviour in a court of law as if they had known each other for years. When Lucas finally insisted they start on the drive back to Tremblant Ashley felt as unwilling to leave as the children had earlier.

She settled back in the car with a sigh of content. The roadway came to meet them like an unwinding spool of white ribbon. 'I love your family, Lucas,' she sighed happily. 'Your father . . . and Philippe. He's such fun!'

'Yeah!' Her sensitive ear noted a morose tone in Lucas's usually vibrant way of speaking, but she decided not to comment on it.

They drove several miles in stony silence. She stole sidelong glances at him from under her lashes. His face looked set and hawklike in the dim interior of the car. Finally, when she felt she would stifle with the tension, she spoke up.

'All right, darling,' she said, 'out with it! What's bothering you?' She sounded calm enough, but her heart was beginning to beat in a very uncomfortable fashion.

He pulled over to the shoulder of the road, and switching off the engine turned to face her. His hands still gripped the steering wheel. 'Do you realise how old I am, Red?' Dumbfounded, she nodded at him, a chestnut curl falling over her smooth forehead. 'I'm thirty-four. And you're not twenty-one yet.' He peered miserably out of the windshield.

'Lucas, you've always known my age,' she protested. 'What's got into you?'

He ran his fingers despairingly through his thick black hair. 'Seeing you with Philippe tonight,' he muttered, 'both of you so young, so *right* together . . . forgive me, Ashley, but I wondered if perhaps . . . perhaps what I *do* blinded you to who I *am*.'

'What are you *talking* about?' she demanded.

'Ashley, I'm not saying you're aware of it, but I wondered if the . . . the glamour . . . of being a well-known movie director was perhaps what attracted you to me . . .'

'Lucas, how dare you!' She was now very angry indeed, her eyes bright green.

'You're so lovely, Ashley . . . and it would be quite natural . . .'

'*What* would?' She snapped.

'To love the whole phoney theatrical package . . . and not see me very clearly. *Me*, Lucas Martineaux . . . ageing colonial . . . nuts about a girl years too young for him . . .'

Ashley let out an exasperated sigh. 'I have never heard such a load of old rubbish in my life,' she said heatedly. 'Why on *earth* should you think such a thing?'

'It happened once before,' he replied bitterly.

In the silence that followed Ashley looked at Lucas, and Lucas kept staring intently at the white-blanketed countryside surrounding them. There was very little traffic on the autoroute to the Laurentians. Sometimes a car sped past, its headlights sweeping across them briefly, but mostly it was quiet. At last Ashley spoke.

'What did Sloane do to you, Lucas, all those years ago?' For she realised, with a sudden flash of intuition, that Sloane had again come between them.

He dropped his hands from the wheel and turned to her at last. 'I was twenty-four . . . Philippe's age . . . Sloane was four years younger. We were engaged to be married. Then she met a fully-fledged director . . . I was still working my way up the ladder. I read about their marriage in the newspaper . . . she didn't even have the decency to tell me herself.'

'*Marriage*? Sloane's *married*?'

'Not any more. It lasted two years, then she ditched him. Discovered he'd become a has-been, no more use to her career.'

'Why do you use her in your film, then, if she behaved so dreadfully?' This disclosure of Lucas's hurt her deeply. She hated to think of him engaged to Sloane.

'Because she's the ideal actress for the role . . . and it's ten years ago. Blood under the bridge! I've got a picture to make, Ashley, that's my prime concern,' Lucas said harshly.

'I see. And you think I'm using you too . . . like she did, is that it?' Ashley felt as if she were being physically beaten.

'Oh God!' Lucas leaned over the steering wheel, his head in his hands. 'Ashley sweetheart, try to understand . . . I love you with all my heart, but it just seems *too* good sometimes . . . and I get scared. I swore ten years ago never to allow myself to trust an actress, never to let myself be made such a fool of again.' He raised his head, his face a mask of hurt masculine pride. 'And then you came along and I knew I was doing all those things I'd sworn not to do, because I love you Ashley . . . if I lose you . . .' His eyes grew suspiciously bright. He drew a deep breath and regained his control. 'I'm a prize idiot,' he went on in a more normal voice, 'seeing you with Philippe tonight, both of you so young . . . I suddenly thought that perhaps, unwittingly, you loved the film director, not the man.'

'What do I have to do to prove myself to you, Lucas?' she asked quietly.

'Be patient. Forgive me for outbursts like this,' his mouth twisted into a weary smile, 'understand that I'm still finding it hard to believe I've been this lucky.'

Ashley leaned across and placed her hands on either side of his troubled face. 'The only thing I want from you is your trust, Lucas,' she said, her grey eyes steady.

He removed her hands and slowly kissed each palm. 'We better get back, honey . . . tomorrow's a working day,' was all he said, but the hurt had left him, she could tell.

For the remainder of the journey she thought over what he had told her, and she realised that she had been foolish earlier to imagine nothing could ever come between them. For in spite of the depth of feeling between them, Lucas was still wary, and only time could prove her loyalty, and cure his distrust.

CHAPTER TEN

THE days left in Tremblant melted away like snow in warm sunshine, and before Ashley had time to catch her breath the location work was completed and they had to return to Toronto for the remainder of the shot.

There had been no recurrence of the scene she had had with Lucas on their way back from Montreal. Indeed, she felt closer to him than ever; as if an invisible thread joined them, so that even though she had few moments alone with him, nevertheless she had the feeling of being exclusively in his company even in a crowd.

This feeling was reinforced since Sloane appeared to have found herself a new man. She had been spending every spare moment at L'Esterel with him.

Their last evening in Tremblant, Lucas and Ashley were in the bar having a nightcap with Maggy when Sloane made one of her spectacular entrances. She looked magnificent in a silk jersey dinner gown of vivid scarlet. Barbaric gold discs hung from her ears. Her thick black hair was twisted into a shining knot low on her neck, pinned with a heavy gold hairpin. She dragged her mink coat behind her as casually as if it were an old cardigan. She was escorted by a fleshy middle-aged man, who shouldered his way to the bar and imperiously ordered a bottle of iced champagne.

'We won't drink it here, Claude,' Sloane announced, 'it's much cosier *chez moi*.' She waved her fingers vaguely at Lucas. 'Hello, darling,' she said, pointedly ignoring Ashley and Maggy, 'you know Claude White, don't you?'

'No. But I've *heard* of Mr White, of course,' Lucas replied pleasantly, nodding to Sloane's portly friend, who favoured the group with a regal stare.

Lucas introduced Ashley and Maggy, since Sloane

obviously wasn't going to. Several aimless remarks were passed concerning the state of the ski slopes, and how the film had been progressing, then Mr White and Sloane left carrying their champagne.

'Wow!' Maggy giggled when they had disappeared, 'she's really landed a big fish this time!'

'Now, now, Maggy! We shouldn't jump to conclusions. He's probably just an acquaintance,' said Lucas, but his expressive eye-brows were raised nonetheless.

'Acquaintances don't buy bottles of Veuve Cliquot to drink *chez moi*,' Maggy pointed out.

Ashley sipped her Irish Cream liqueur. 'I take it Mr White is quite somebody, the way you're both carrying on,' she observed.

'My dear innocent girl!' Lucas patted her hand. 'Claude White is a financier—one of the wealthiest, if not in the world, certainly in North America.'

'And La Sheppard's not averse to money or power,' Maggy interrupted, 'both of which Claude White has in spades.'

'Well, I for one wish her luck,' said Lucas, taking Ashley's hand and melting her with a look. 'If Sloane's half as happy as I am these days she's rich indeed.'

Nothing more was said about Sloane and her financier friend that evening. Still Ashley felt a sense of relief, for if Sloane was involved with someone else, particularly someone as important as this man, surely she would be less inclined to hold a grudge, or try to make trouble.

When they returned to Toronto Ashley found mail waiting for her at the hotel including a long, loving letter from Auntie Con, blessing her for the money she had sent them and filling her in on news of the village. As she read her letter while looking at the black waters of Lake Ontario, the Cotswold cottage seemed a lifetime away.

Ashley hadn't written home about Lucas. The pressure of work had left her little time for letter writing. A few postcards to let them know she was well and busy had been all she had had time for. Besides, she wanted to tell them about him in person, for she felt she could never adequately describe him, or the happiness she felt with him, in a letter. In any case they would be seeing him for themselves soon, since there were only a few days left to work on the picture. Then she would be flying back to England followed by Lucas, who had promised to join her there as soon as he could. She longed to introduce him to her mother and her aunt, for she suspected Lucas and Aunt Constance would hit it off right away.

The work in Toronto was not as uncomfortable as it had been in Tremblant, for here they were either in the studio or at Casa Loma Castle. But the hours were long. For this part of the movie Ashley had to be beautifully groomed and coiffured, which meant being in the make-up room at five a.m.; so that by the time she finished work at six she was very tired indeed.

Sloane's schedule was much easier, but she was also tired, though for a different reason. Claude White had followed her to Toronto, and now the gossip columns carried stories and pictures of the financier wining and dining the exotic movie star in various plush night spots. She managed to still look glamorous and groomed in the morning when she had to work, but her temper was waspish to say the least, and her popularity with the crew took a further nosedive.

The pace of work accelerated as they got closer to the end of the film. By now Ashley felt as at home on the floor of the set as she had on stage. And she realised that not only had she been able to bail the family out of its financial troubles, and discovered the joy of Lucas's love, as an added plus she had mastered another facet of her craft.

The final scene was shot late one evening, and when the first A.D. called it a wrap the crew and the actors broke up amid hugs and handshakes, accompanied by the usual feeling of anticlimax that occurs at the finish of any venture of this kind. It had been announced pre-viously that the wrap party would not be held for another three days because Lucas had to go to New York for meetings with the stage designer of *King Lear*. Ashley was not going with him since his schedule promised to be hectic.

The night of the final wrap Lucas took her out for a late dinner at Fenton's Restaurant to celebrate. They ate in the Garden—a glass-domed room riotous with trees in brick tubs, trained vines overhead, and a long table against one wall crowded with baskets of fruit and vegetables and a mass of bright pots of hyacinth, narcissus, and daffodils.

Lucas had changed from his working uniform of jeans and casual shirt and looked elegant in a black silk suit and snowy white shirt. His hair had been smoothed down and glinted blue-black in the candlelight.

'I hate leaving you behind, Red,' he said, he was leaving the following morning, 'but I can't get out of this New York junket.'

'It's only three days, darling.' Ashley took a sip of her wine. 'I plan to sleep late in the mornings, and I've several auditions too . . . I'd like to work on this side of the Atlantic again . . . I'm seeing people at the CBC, and some theatre producers . . .'

'You know you can use my name, honey,' he said. 'Who are you seeing at the CBC? It's probably someone I know.'

She played with the slender stem of her glass. Now that the film was over she had painted her pretty oval nails pink to match her lipstick. 'I'll certainly tell them I've just finished working for you, Lucas,' she told him, 'but I won't ride on your name . . . as your girl-friend,' she raised her eyes to meet his. 'I'll do it on my own, Lucas.'

'My free-spirited redhead, eh?' he said ironically. But she divined the admiration that lay behind this remark, and knew she had said the right thing.

They went to a night-club in Yorkville and danced till dawn. Not that either of them was fond of night-clubs, but they couldn't bear to part. They danced silently, Lucas holding her close, until the club closed, and when he kissed her goodbye the sun was sending long fingers of rosy light through the windows of her hotel room.

'I'll see you in three days, my darling,' he said, stroking her cheek with his fingers, 'and I'll phone when I can.' He kissed her willing mouth once more, then gently pushed her away from him. 'And don't wear that dress while I'm gone.' She was wearing her striped grey and white cotton dress.

'Oh, don't you like it?'

'Like it? It's dynamite! Only to be worn in my presence. Now go to bed before you fall asleep on your feet.'

Ashley slept till noon. She was drugged with fatigue and happiness. Her first appointment wasn't until late afternoon, so she had plenty of time to wash and dry her thick hair before leaving. A large box of gardenias was delivered before she went out. The accompanying note read: 'A few gardenias from the glade I promised you. Each of these flowers is a kiss between us. L.' She buried her rosy face in their delicate waxen petals. They were heavy with fragrance, and a wave of love and longing for Lucas swept over her.

Her audition went well, as far as she could judge from the neutral manner of the C.B.C. casting director. When she returned to her room, heavily perfumed now from Lucas's flowers, she was suddenly very drowsy, so she stretched out on the bed and slept. The phone woke her. She opened her eyes and reached for the receiver in one movement, convinced it would be Lucas on the other end of the line. It wasn't. A strange male voice greeted her.

'Ashley Morrison?' She identified herself groggily.

'My name's Alan Carfox. I'm with the magazine *Entertaining World*.'

'Ye-yes?' She'd seen the magazine on the stands.

'We're doing a series of articles on actors visiting us from other countries. I wondered if you'd grant me an interview?'

'Well, I . . .' She was still heavy with sleep.

'I'm in the lobby. It'll only take a few minutes. I'll meet you in the Quayside Lounge. Bring a picture.'

'How will I know you?' asked Ashley, bewildered, her mind not functioning properly yet.

'You won't. I'll know you, though. You've got red hair, haven't you? See you in ten minutes. OK?'

'Just a minute, I . . .' But he had hung up. Ashley peered at her travelling clock. It was nearly seven.

She splashed her face with cold water and combed out her thick hair. An article on visiting actors sounded reasonable enough—and yet her instinct was sending out warnings; she hadn't liked Mr Carfox's voice, or his manner. But, she told herself, he was a reporter. Brash behaviour was probably second nature to him.

'The trouble with me is, I'm tired,' she said aloud. But even as she was going down in the elevator she couldn't shake off a sense of foreboding that seemed to press against the windows with the night.

She took an instant dislike to Alan Carfox. He was a heavy-set young man whose clothes were a little too tight, and whose hair was a little too oily. His pallid face shone as if it had been buttered. He overrode her refusal of a rye and ginger.

'Aw, c'mon. I'm having one,' he said. 'I don't like to drink alone.' A statement she doubted, judging from his alcoholic breath.

When the drinks arrived he downed his in one gulp, and producing a notebook and pen proceeded with the interview. His question seemed innocuous enough, even boring—what did she think of the weather in Canada? Of the food? Were the working conditions on the film similar to those in England?

'I can't answer that,' she pointed out. 'I've never made a movie before.'

'Is that a fact?' His red-rimmed eyes regarded her. 'How come you landed such a juicy part, then?'

'Mr Martineaux saw me perform in a play in London and offered me the role,' she replied, endeavouring to keep the edge out of her voice.

'Quite a lucky break.'

'Yes.'

'How d'you like working with Martineaux?' he asked,

inspecting his empty glass and summoning the waiter.

'He's wonderful to work for. A very talented man.' She pushed her untasted rye towards him. 'Here, have mine. I told you I didn't want one.'

'You sure are unsociable,' he said, taking her drink nevertheless. Ashley noticed that his hand trembled, and it didn't take much imagination to figure out that Alan Carfox had a drinking problem.

'I think it's unsociable to force drinks on people who don't want them, frankly,' she said. She was finding this oaf more and more offensive.

He looked at her truculently for a minute, then appeared to think better of it. 'Yeah!' He swallowed a mouthful of rye. 'Are you going to be in Martineaux's production of *Lear*?' he threw at her.

This was so unexpected that she stammered, as if unsure of her answer. 'Why, I . . . No . . . no.'

'Has he finished casting, then?' His goose-blue eyes never left her face.

'No . . . at least, I don't know . . .'

'So you *could* be in it?'

'I've never thought about it . . . I mean . . . we've never discussed it.'

'There's a part for you in it, though, isn't there?' He persisted. 'One of Lear's daughters is in your age range, isn't she?'

'Cordelia? Well, yes, but . . .'

'I mean, most young actresses would kill for a chance to play that part on Broadway, wouldn't they?'

'I suppose so . . . but I really must . . .' Ashley suddenly wanted to get away from this barrage of questions.

'Particularly since you'd be working with a director you admire. You *did* say you thought Martineaux was talented?'

'He is. He's wonderful . . . but . . .' She felt inexplicably cornered.

'Is it true you and Martineaux are romantically involved?'

'Wh-what?'

He leaned his sweaty face close to hers. 'You and Martineaux. I've heard you're a twosome.'

'That has nothing whatever to do with you . . . or with this article!' Ashley was trembling with anger.

'That means you are,' he said triumphantly, 'or you wouldn't be so upset.'

Ashley was beginning to feel frightened. 'Mr Carfox, I must *insist* you don't print anything like that in your article,' she said.

'Relax, sweetie. Our readers aren't interested in that kinda stuff,' he assured her. But she persisted.

'You said you wanted to get my impressions of this country, and I agreed to that . . . nothing else.'

'OK, OK, calm down. Have a drink.'

'No, thank you.' She got up. 'I don't want to talk to you any more, Mr Carfox.'

'Suit yourself. It's no skin off my nose!' He waved a stubby-fingered hand dismissively. 'Thanks for giving me your *valuable* time.' he turned away and beckoned the waiter for another drink. 'I'll just have a coupla drinks before I make tracks,' he smiled blearily into her anxious face. 'Class dismissed!'

Ashley wished him a frosty goodnight and returned to her room, filled with a mixture of fatigue and apprehension. She would have given anything for Lucas to have been there. She missed his steadying presence even more than she had realised. Deciding to forgo dinner, she had a long hot bath and an early night.

After a good night's sleep the anxiety she had suffered receded, and though the memory of the obnoxious Alan Carfox still made her shudder, she thought that she had been overreacting last night. She reasoned that she had been very overtired, and no doubt that had been the prime cause for her fears. When Lucas phoned her for a brief call on his way between appointments, she didn't tell him about her interview. She didn't want to waste the few precious minutes talking with him about someone as boring and nasty as Alan Carfox.

After her morning audition she spent the day wandering around Toronto. She discovered Chinatown and browsed happily in the streets that bore Chinese characters beneath their English ones. She ate lunch at the Art Gallery of Ontario, then sat in the large upstairs gallery that housed Toronto's famous Henry Moore sculptures. A diffused light shone through the frosted skylights on to the massive, fluid figures, creating an atmosphere of peace and tranquillity. Later she walked through the Eaton Centre, gazing wide-eyed at the brilliantly lit stores that flanked the fountain, delighted that she was protected from the late afternoons icy drizzle by the vaulted glass roof. She bought herself an ice cream cone from a store that boasted '31 Flavors' to choose from, and treated herself to a pair of diaphanous silver hose, as fine as moonbeams.

Back at the hotel she bumped into Jane and some members of the crew. They joined forces and went for hamburgers followed by a movie, and when she got back to the hotel again there was a message from Maggy, inviting her to spend the following day with her and her young son.

And so the three days of Lucas's absence passed. Not exactly quickly, but pleasantly enough, what with auditions and new friends, and explorations of the charming city.

Lucas phoned her each day, but he was clearly frantically busy and the calls were hurried. It was arranged that he would get back to Toronto in time to pick her up for the wrap party. She had checked with Maggy about proper clothes for this particular occasion and had been assured that unlike the first get-together at the start of the film, this was a formal affair. She decided to really dress up, so that Lucas would be provoked into remarking upon her extravagance once again. Then she would tell him about her clever dressmaker aunt and the financial crisis at home, and all would be happily explained.

There was one gown Aunt Constance had made for her that she had not had a chance to wear. In fact they had had quite an argument about it when she'd been packing to come to Canada, since Ashley was convinced she would never have any occasion to wear such a dress.

'Rubbish, child!' her irascible aunt had exclaimed. 'Every girl should have at least one wicked gown in her luggage!'

Aunt Constance's description was apt. Fashioned from chalk-white crêpe, it was cut on the bias, so that it clung to every curve of Ashley's body without appearing to touch it. The back was low cut, to below the curve of her waist. The bodice swooped revealingly, and the ankle-length skirt was shaped like two petals of a tulip. Demure when she stood still, but slit to her thighs, it showed glimpses of her shapely legs when she walked. She had put on the silver panty-hose she had bought, and was happy to see they were a perfect foil for the heavy white crêpe of her dress. Her only jewellery was her peridot bracelet, and she had threaded some of Lucas's gardenias into her lustrous hair, which curled loosely on her naked shoulders. She splashed herself generously with l'Air du Temps and slipped her narrow feet into high-heeled silver sandals.

There was a peremptory knock at her door, and her heart leapt with joy. This must be Lucas. She had thought he might phone first . . . but it didn't matter, she was so happy to see him again.

She flung the door open and pirouetted so that her skirt billowed out and her slender silver legs glittered. 'Welcome back, dar . . .' One look at his face stopped her in mid-sentence, for he was clearly in a fury. His face blanched, his eyes glittering like shards of mica. He was still wearing his suede topcoat, and carried his overnight case and a folded newspaper.

He stepped into the room, slamming the door behind him. 'Too bad, Ashley,' he said through gritted teeth, 'too bad. You nearly brought it off!'

She stared at him in amazement. 'What are you talking about?'

'You can quit the innocent act—superb though it is,' his lips twisted bitterly.

She clasped her hands together imploringly. 'Please,

Lucas . . . I haven't the faintest idea what you're talking about.'

'You blew it, baby! That's what I'm talking about,' he rasped. He pushed the newspaper into her hands with such force she staggered and nearly fell. 'I'm talking about your publicity in this edition of *Entertaining World*.'

Ashley looked down at the paper in her nerveless hands. In bold black capitals she read: 'UNKNOWN ACTRESS ASHLEY MORRISON LETS LOVE GUIDE HER TO BROADWAY'. And beneath, in smaller letters: 'Any actress would kill for the role, the ambitious redhead declares.'

The print writhed before her eyes like black serpents. 'Oh God! No!' she whispered.

'Put it in too early for you, did they?' Lucas said caustically. 'I guess you thought I'd be safely out of the country by the time your little item hit the press.'

'Oh, Lucas, no! I mean . . .'

But he was in a passion of rage and gave her no chance to defend herself. 'Don't try to deny it. I'm wise now to your little tricks,' he looked at her with loathing. 'It made fascinating reading on the plane, I can tell you. How you're going to play Cordelia in New York . . .'

'*What?*' She felt sick with horror.

'Yeah! And how *useful* it is that on your first movie the *wonderful* Lucas Martineaux fell madly in love with you . . .'

'Oh, Lucas, I never said anything like that!' She tried to touch him, but he turned away from her with a convulsive movement.

'I could kill you for this!' he choked furiously.

'But, Lucas darling, I didn't . . .' Desperately she fought to control her tears.

'*I don't want any more lies!*' he exploded. 'No more play-acting. You're too good at it, Ashley, and I'm too easily taken in. Just answer me one question—just yes or no. Did you give an interview to *Entertaining World* or not?'

'Yes, but . . .'

A muscle twitched in his white face. 'That's all I wanted to know!'

'But, Lucas . . .' she pleaded.

'Don't say any more, or I may hit you,' he snarled. She flinched at the violence in his voice and was unable to suppress a broken sob. 'A very touching performance, Ashley, but it doesn't fool me any more,' he said cruelly, 'so you can cut it out. In fact you can cut out altogether. I'm arranging for you to go back to England on the first available flight. That gives you about an hour to pack.'

'But . . . but the party?' she asked faintly. Not that the party mattered at this point, but it was the first thing that sprang into her dazed mind.

'You won't be going to it. I'll say you've been called home suddenly.'

She looked up at him. Her face rigid with shock, her lips ashen. 'Oh, Lucas . . .'

'No, Ashley! *No*. I want you out of my sight!' Lucas hissed savagely. 'You sicken me!'

She couldn't control her grief any longer. Her eyes brimmed, and tears slid down her cheeks. 'Oh, Lucas . . . please . . .'

'Save that for the camera, Ashley,' he sneered. 'You've got a great future—even without me.' He paused in the doorway. 'I'll leave you the paper. You can put it in your scrapbook, along with your other trophies.'

She stood quite still after he had gone, the paper still clutched in her hand. Then a storm of weeping swept over her and the hateful article fell to the carpeted floor while she leant against the wall in a paroxysm of despair. She was trapped in a nightmare. Only no matter how hard she sobbed she couldn't wake up.

When her crying stopped she picked up the paper and read Alan Carfox's article. It was more damning than she had imagined. He had not only twisted everything she had said, but had presented her in such a way as to make her appear a hard opportunist, using Lucas's love as a ladder for her ambition. Bewildered, she crushed the offensive thing to a ball and hurled it into the wastebasket.

Why would Carfox write such an article? It was true they had disliked each other, but to perpetrate such a character assassination? It didn't make sense. But she was too full of misery to pursue this further.

Suddenly her phone rang. She hurried to answer it, believing for one wild moment that it must be Lucas to tell her the whole thing had been a horrifying misunderstanding. But it wasn't Lucas. It was the desk clerk to confirm that she was booked on that night's last flight to London.

Numbly she took off her beautiful white dress and started to pack. The sight of the gardenias threaded through her hair almost started her tears flowing again, but she controlled herself and finished folding her things with automatic precision.

Before she left she put the peridots into their velvet box and sealed them in an envelope. This she left at the desk to be delivered to Lucas. She didn't include any note . . . what was the use? She realised he was too hurt and angry to believe anything she might say.

She saved one of the gardenias and held it tightly in her hand during the long flight home. Its petals were as faded and dead as her happiness. A cruel reminder of yesterday's dream.

CHAPTER ELEVEN

SHE arrived at Heathrow to find the airport in an uproar. The airport buses were on strike and taxis were practically unobtainable. Not that Ashley could have afforded a taxi—even a shared one—all the way to London. So she sat in the arrivals lounge until a reasonable hour and then phoned an S.O.S. to Gus, who willingly offered to drive in and pick her up.

She waited for him, sitting beside her luggage, her back ramrod-straight, staring intently ahead, but not seeing the crowd milling around her. When she focused her eyes at last, the fat figure of Gus was standing in front of her, a smile of welcome on his face.

'Here we are then, my dove, all safe and accounted for!' He bestowed an avuncular kiss on her pale cheek. 'What a welcome, eh!' He indicated the mass of humanity scrambling for taxis. 'I don't know what the country's coming to.'

Ashley gave him the ghost of a smile. 'You're a lifesaver, Gus. A knight in shining armour.'

'Well,. I don't know about that, poppet. After all, you've been slaving on that film for the past six weeks. Being met at the airport seems the very least you can expect,' he bent down and picked up her heaviest suitcase. 'Blimey, what did you pack in this, my petal? Bricks?' She went to help him, but he genially waved her away. 'No . . . no, I'll manage. Just balance me on the other side with one of the others, otherwise I'm liable to keel over . . . There, that's the ticket! The car's not far. Let's get out of this mob.'

Ashley followed him mutely, too sunk in her personal misery to pay attention to the jostling crowd. She was using every ounce of self-control not to break down under Gus's affectionate banter. She didn't want to burden him with her troubles. What would be the point?

He could do nothing to bring Lucas back to her, and that was the only thing that could stop the bitter tears that clogged her throat and threatened to fall from her sad grey eyes.

Once they were heading towards London Gus relaxed behind the wheel. 'Aren't you back sooner than you said, my lamb?' He asked.

She looked out of the side window, not wanting him to see her face. 'We finished ahead of schedule,' she lied brightly, 'there didn't seem to be any point hanging around.'

'Still, you could have cabled you was coming,' Gus said reasonably, 'then I'd have been waiting to meet you.'

'I never thought of it.' She stared hard at the houses flashing past. They seemed so small after Canada. Everything looked strange to her now. She wondered hopelessly if she would ever feel at home here again. Or happy.

'Well, you done all right on that film,' Gus went on blithely. 'You made a right packet, my treasure. And with the experience of working for a director like Lucas Martineaux we should be able to sit back and wait for the offers to come flooding in.'

'Good,' she replied, her voice muffled with tears. It was hearing Gus say Lucas's name that did it. Up till now she had managed to hold her tears at bay.

'Are you all right, my angel?'

'Just tired,' she said. 'I . . . I didn't sleep on the plane.' The tears slid down her cheeks, tasting salty on her lips. She fumbled in her bag for a handkerchief. 'Blast! I . . . I'm sorry, Gus.'

He threw her a sidelong glance. 'That's what agents are for,' he teased, 'to be used like wailing walls.' He waited while she blew her nose. 'You're not worried about the film, are you, Ashley? About your perform-ance, I mean.'

'N-no.' She dabbed at her eyes, still beautiful if red-rimmed.

'Cos I know you was a success. Martineaux sent word

that he thought you was fantastic.'

Hope flickered briefly. 'When was that?'

''Bout four weeks ago.'

'Oh!' She gulped miserably.

'You know what you should do, duckie?' Gus said kindly. 'You should take a bit of a holiday. You're regular done in.'

'Y-yes.'

'Go and stay with your mum for a bit. I won't let on to *nobody* where you are, no matter what comes up. Just forget about work for a couple of weeks. Go into hiding like.'

'Yes . . . yes, I think I will.' Indeed Gus's suggestion did appeal to her. She longed for the solace of the country. She gave him a watery smile. 'Thanks, Gus.'

'Just being practical, my lovey. You're a hot property since this film. Got to keep you fit—stands to reason.'

For the rest of the journey Ashley continued to stare mutely out of the car window. A 'hot property'! She should be feeling delighted, it was every young actress's dream . . . to be sought after, to have offers flooding in . . . but all she could think of was the contempt in Lucas's eyes when he had told her to get out of his sight. That contempt would surely be reinforced when she started making a name for herself on the strength of her performance in his movie. He would go on thinking she had lied and used him, and never really loved him at all. That was what hurt so terribly . . . that he could believe her capable of such deceit. That pain was almost worse than the pain of losing him.

She left for the Cotswolds the following day. She was determined not to let Aunt Constance or her mother know anything of her unhappiness. She particularly wanted to shield her mother from any distress, so she made much of being exhausted from her six weeks' filming, and prayed they would accept that as an excuse for her silence and lack of appetite.

She had not reckoned with her aunt. Her first night home she was sitting with that lady drinking a mug of cocoa before the dying fire. Both of them were in their

dressing-gowns ready for bed. Muppet's head lay ador-
ingly across Ashley's slippered feet. Ashley had been
gazing into the embers, trying not to think how different
her homecoming would have been if that pernicious
article had never been printed, when Aunt Constance
put aside her inevitable sewing and peered at her niece
over her glasses.

'Do you want to talk about it, Ashley?' she asked
softly.

Startled, Ashley's huge grey eyes, shadowed with
grief, left their examination of the fire and looked into
Aunt Connie's blue ones. 'Wh—what do you mean,
Auntie?'

'Oh, come, my dear! It's plain something's happened.
Why else would you be moping around like a moon-
struck hedgehog?'

In spite of her misery Ashley smiled at her aunt's
peculiar analogy. 'I'm just tired, darling.'

'I may be getting on, but I'm not *daft*, child,' snapped
her aunt, then she continued in a gentler tone: 'If you
don't want to talk about it, Ashley, I won't press you.
But you do know that if you need to unburden yourself,
I'm here.'

Ashley put her hand on her aunt's bony, flannel-
covered knee. 'Yes, darling, I know. I don't mean to
mope. It's just that I can't talk about it . . . not yet,' she
faltered, 'it . . . it hurts too much.'

Aunt Constance covered Ashley's slim hand with her
gnarled one. 'I won't pry my dear,' she muttered, 'just
answer me one thing,' she looked intently into her
niece's wistful face. 'Is he worth all this agony?'

A sad smile flickered round Ashley's childlike mouth.
'How do you know it's a man that's making me unhappy?' she asked.

'Because it usually is!' her aunt snorted. 'I just want to
know if he's worth it.'

Ashley answered her steadily. 'He's worth it,' she
said. Her clear gaze never faltered.

'I was afraid of that,' the older woman sighed. 'I don't
see you breaking your heart over second-best.'

After that the subject was never mentioned again. Aunt Constance kept her busy with a dozen chores, presumably in an effort to keep her mind off her troubles. It worked up to a point. But the pain never left her. She had never realised before that unhappiness was an actual physical pain. Like a small lump of lead resting in the middle of her chest, a dull, sad ache that kept her locked in grief.

About ten days into her stay she woke to find the fields washed in delicate spring sunshine. The sky was bird's-egg blue, and fat white clouds chased each other in the stringent wind. After breakfast Aunt Constance persuaded Ashley to take Muppet and go for a long walk.

'Why don't you go to Little Hollow and bring us back some primroses?' her mother suggested. 'They should be out by now.'

So, when the breakfast dishes were dried, Ashley, accompanied by her bounding dog, set off for the spinney. It was indeed a glorious spring day. The trees were misted with buds, like pale green dust, and wild daffodils scattered the fresh meadows. To Ashley they were like arrows piercing her heart, for they reminded her cruelly of her dinner with Lucas at Fenton's Garden Restaurant, where the pots of forced spring flowers had glowed so bravely on the long table, and had seemed to echo the promise that life seemed to offer then.

Little Hollow was set in the centre of the spinney like a bowl. It had always been one of Ashley's favourite places. As a child she had delighted to crouch in the very centre of it, looking up at the trees that edged its perfect circular rim. And it was a great place for wild flowers. White and purple violets were to be found hiding under blankets of dead leaves, crocus gaily spread out of the rich earth near the boles of small saplings that dotted the steep incline. And primroses, pale as fresh butter, grew in profusion. But to Ashley it was as if all colour had been drained from the world. The sky, the trees, even the vivid crocus, all were flat, dreary grey.

She filled her basket with primroses, covered them with damp leaves to keep them fresh, then sat on a fallen log, while Muppet thrust himself between her knees, and anxiously tried to lick her face.

Ashley caressed his rough head. 'Oh, Muppet, Muppet . . . I'm so miserable!' she confided to her canine friend, hugging him close. Two tears dripped on to her hand, and she let go of the squirming dog to search in the pocket of her jeans for a handkerchief.

'Red . . . *Red*! Where are you?'

The hair rose on the back of her neck, for even though it was faint, she could have sworn that it was Lucas's voice that was being carried to her by the wind.

She heard it again—closer this time. 'Red, please, Red, tell me where you are!'

Slowly she got to her feet, her heart beating painfully. Muppet, his ears pointed, started to growl . . . so she wasn't dreaming . . . Muppet heard Lucas too. Then she saw him. He stood on the edge of Little Hollow, his tall figure silhouetted against the blue sky.

Muppet, his wagging tail contradicting his volley of excited barks, danced round in a circle, noisily protecting his young mistress. Alerted by the dog's clamour, Lucas looked down into the shadows of the Hollow and saw her.

'Ashley . . . Ashley!' he cried, sliding rapidly down the steep slope. He halted in a shower of dead leaves and stood about six feet from her. She remained motionless, her coppery hair blazing against the dark foliage. Her eyes were wide with wonder. 'Hello, Red,' he said softly. He searched her still face.

Ashley found her voice. 'What . . . what are you doing here?'

'Looking for you. You left something behind.' He held out his hand, and looped through his long fingers she saw the green watery fire of the peridots. She made no move to take them, but stood like a marble statue in the shadowy wood. Lucas stepped closer and dropped the bracelet into the basket of primroses. It lay on the yellow petals like smooth drops of water.

She noted that his face looked drawn, the craggy lines etched deeper. 'I didn't come only to return your bracelet,' he said. 'I came to ask you . . . to beg you . . . to forgive me. Can you?'

'I . . . I don't know, Lucas,' she answered, her beautiful voice tight. 'I want to . . . but if you believe I'd say, even *think* the things that Carfox wrote in that article . . .'

'Oh, Ashley—I was mad! Insane. I know I'm asking a lot . . . but just try to understand. It was as if the past was repeating itself . . . mocking me. In my heart I knew you weren't like that, but when I first read that . . . that filth, I went mad for a while. My dreadful temper . . .' He stood before her, his face a mask of contrition.

'And now, Lucas?' She regarded him sombrely. 'Do you still believe I said those things?'

'I know for a fact that you didn't,' he replied. 'I realised how unjust I'd been as soon as I regained my sanity—but by then you'd left, and I couldn't find you.'

'Oh, Lucas . . . Lucas . . . !' Her iron reserve broke, and her tears fell unchecked. She made no attempt to wipe them away. He swept her into his arms and held her fiercely, raining kisses on her wet cheeks, her eyelids, her tangled hair.

'Sh, sweetheart . . . sweetheart, don't! Don't cry,' he murmured brokenly, 'I can't bear to see you cry.'

Her storm of weeping subsided at last and she stood quietly in the haven of his embrace in a dream of reawakened happiness. The feel of his arms around her, the smell of his skin, was a bliss she thought she had lost for ever.

Upset by his mistress's distress, Muppet whined and pawed Ashley to get her attention. She reluctantly freed herself from Lucas and patted the dog. 'It's all right, Muppet . . . good dog . . . it's all right,' she reassured the animal.

'Does he bite men who kiss you?' Lucas asked, with a touch of his old teasing manner.

She smiled up at him, her cheeks regaining their former glow through the tearstains. 'I don't know. He's never seen me being kissed before.'

'I'm delighted to hear that.' He knelt beside her and

stroked Muppet's head. 'You'd better get used to it, old fellow,' he said, 'I plan to make a habit of it.'

To demonstrate his point he took her into his arms again and claimed her unresisting mouth. With a sigh Ashley wound her arms around his neck and gave herself voluptuously to the delight of feeling his warm lips caressing hers. They fell back on to the soft carpet of leaves, and she clung to him, feeling his body hard against hers.

Eventually Lucas relinquished her mouth, and pushing his fingers through her thick russet mane pulled her head gently backwards. 'I think we'd better go and sit on that log over there,' he suggested huskily. 'I can't hold you like that much longer without possessing you utterly.'

'I know,' she answered throatily, twining her arms around him again. 'I feel the same.'

'Help me to behave myself, you delicious wanton,' he chided, unwillingly dragging them both to their feet. 'You'll shock Muppet!'

He seated her on the mossy log, and sat beside her. The pale spring sunshine dappled them with shimmering discs of light.

'I've several things to ask you, honey,' he said, 'and I've still got a lot of explaining to do . . .'

'Yes,' she exclaimed, 'for instance . . . how on earth did you find me?' For until this moment she had been too delighted by his reappearance in her life to question how he got there.

'Thereby hangs a tale!' Lucas said ironically. 'Well, I went to the wrap party and . . . I'm not very proud of myself, Ashley . . . I had several large drinks very quickly, and I began to feel even more dreadful than I had before.' He looked at her gravely. 'I don't appear in a very good light, my sweet,' he went on, 'but you must know that I've never done such a thing before . . . and I'm not a drinker. But everyone kept asking where you were, and I was in such agony . . . anyway, Maggy finally took me to one side and asked me what was bugging me . . . and I told her the whole story, and how I'd sent you away. She gave me hell!' He smiled grimly at the memory. 'She bundled me into her car then and there, and drove me to the airport. But your plane had gone . . . that sobered me up in a hurry, I can tell you.'

'You came to . . . to bring me back?' Ashley asked tremulously.

He nodded. 'By force if I had to. But I was too late. So next morning I cabled your agent asking for your address in London. Then I decided to get to the bottom of the interview business, so I went round to the offices of *Entertaining World* and had a . . . a talk . . . with Mr Carfox.' Lucas flexed the knuckles of his left hand at the memory of that encounter.

'Oh, Lucas! Did you . . . did you *hit* him?'

'I didn't need to. All I did was threaten to hit him, and he admitted that it was a set-up. That he'd been bribed by Sloane.'

'By *Sloane*!' Ashley cried out, startled. 'But *why*? What possible reason could she have to do such a thing?'

'Ah, my sweet innocent!' Lucas ran his fingers through his black curls in that familiar gesture she loved so well. 'She did it because she's eaten up with jealousy of you.'

'Of *me*?' She found it incredible that famous Sloane Sheppard could be jealous of a beginner.

'Don't underestimate yourself, Ashley,' he told her softly. 'You're beautiful and talented. Two things calculated to upset Sloane very much. I've been so *blind*!' he exclaimed. 'I'd forgotten what a dangerous woman she is. I should have realised that she was smouldering with jealousy all through the shoot. She never could stand competition. And you're just brimming with talent and . . . with *starfire* . . . you light up the screen. She couldn't bear that.'

'But what was the point of bribing Alan Carfox to write such an article?' she asked.

'To discredit you in my eyes. Remember she also felt I'd rejected her because of you.'

'But Claude White . . . what about him?'

'I think he's just another man she's using for her own

selfish ends. Don't forget the old saying . . . "Hell hath no fury like a movie star scorned".'

'Poor Sloane,' Ashley said thoughtfully, 'she must be dreadfully insecure to behave like that.'

'Save your sympathy, Red,' advised Lucas, 'Sloane will survive—even after the bawling-out I gave her.'

She looked at his set jaw and shivered. 'You saw Sloane after you'd found out what she'd done?'

'Uh-huh!' His eyes grew reflective, 'I think I succeeded in terrifying her,' he said. 'She won't bother you again.' He picked up a stick and threw it for Muppet before resuming.

'The next day there was a cable from your agent saying that he wasn't authorised to give me your home address.'

'Dear Gus,' she smiled, 'he wanted me to have a holiday undisturbed.'

'Dear Gus, indeed!' Lucas snorted. 'I could have wrung his neck! I sent off a second cable explaining that I *had* to get in touch with you, and offering you the part of Cordelia in *Lear*.'

'*What*?' Her eyes became green with surprise.

'Oh, honey! I wanted you to play it from the start,' he said.

'You *did*! Why on earth didn't you tell me?'

'Because I wanted you to give your undivided attention to the film,' he explained patiently. 'I didn't want your concentration diverted. I planned to ask you to play it the night of the wrap party, among other things . . . as a surprise.'

'It's a surprise all right,' she said. 'I had no idea.'

'Will you do it, Red? You're dead right for Cordelia. And we'd be working together again . . .'

Bewildered, Ashley nodded her head. 'Well, yes, of course, darling . . . it's,' she smiled wickedly, 'it's a part any young actress would kill for!'

'Yeah!' Lucas grinned ruefully. 'Well, after I'd sent off the second cable, there was nothing more I could do, so I set to work with the editing of *Time of Trial* . . . which was aptly named in the circumstances.' He let out a long sigh. 'It was agony, Red—seeing you on the screen, and believing I'd lost you. I was punished for my foolishness then, I promise you.'

She hugged him and lightly kissed his lean brown cheek. 'It's in the past, Lucas darling. Forget it now.'

'I'll try, honey, but nearly losing you that way . . . hurting you so . . . it haunts me.' He put his arm round her shoulder and squeezed hard. 'I didn't get a reply to that cable for two days,' he went on, 'by which time I was a nervous wreck! And when it did arrive it still didn't tell me where to find you—merely said you were vacationing for two weeks and that your agent would get in touch with me when you returned. So I decided to come over to England and find you myself. I finished my part of the editing as fast as I could and caught the first plane out.'

'When did you arrive?' she asked.

'This morning early. I went straight to a phone booth and pored through all the Morrisons in the phone directory.'

'I'm not in the London phone book,' she said, 'I use the pay-phone where I live.'

'You're telling me!' he exploded. 'I practically *memorised* that bloody book! And I called so many wrong numbers I thought I'd get deported. Do you know how many A. Morrisons there *are* listed in the London Directory?' Ashley giggled helplessly. 'After the most frustrating two hours of my life I went to see your agent and threw myself on his mercy.'

'And Gus gave you my address here?'

'Only after I'd told him the whole story, and explained what an idiot I'd been.'

'Dear Gus!' she smiled warmly. Lucas quickly kissed the dimple at the corner of her mouth.

'Gus wants to know if he can give you away,' he said. 'Providing, of course, you agree to marry me.'

'Oh, Lucas! *Darling.*' Her beautiful grey eyes answered his question, and he kissed her again, lingeringly.

'I bought this when I was in New York,' he said at last, bringing a small jewellery box out of his jacket pocket. He opened the lid and a half-hoop of diamonds sparkled in the sunshine. 'I planned to ask you at the wrap party,' he told her wryly, slipping the ring on to her finger. 'But I only want a very short engagement, Red. Just long enough to make the arrangements and fly my family over for the wedding . . .'

'Oh, Lucas! Would they come?'

'Just try keeping them away! But we should be able to do all that in a couple of weeks . . .'

'A couple of *weeks*!' Ashley laughed, holding up her hand to admire her ring.

'I haven't the patience to wait any longer, Red,' he told her seriously. 'I want a long honeymoon—maybe a cruise—before we start work on *Lear*. We'll get a special licence if we have to . . .'

'Yes, Lucas, yes! I'll marry you tomorrow if you want!' She was bubbling with joy, but he remained solemn.

'I need you, Ashley,' he said. 'I've always wanted to look after you, and protect you—and I will—but since this last business . . . I've come to see that I *need* you too . . . to give me ballast in my life . . . a rock in this crazy, mixed-up profession we've chosen. I think we'll make a great team, sweetheart, both in our work and in our marriage. And I won't have us working for long periods away from each other. That's no life. How can you keep a proper relationship alive, if each partner is the other side of the world for most of the time? I wouldn't want that for us. I want to build a home with you. That has to come before our careers. You want that too, Ashley . . . don't you?'

She reached for his hands and held them tight. 'Yes, my darling . . . I want it more than anything else. The glamour . . . it's hollow, meaningless, without the rock of our love to build on.'

Lucas freed his hand and smoothed back her silky red hair. 'And children, Ashley? I want a family with you.'

She leaned her cheek against his caressing hand. 'There's nothing I want more, Lucas,' she assured him.

'And we must tell each other what's in our hearts, Ashley,' he said earnestly. 'No more keeping things back. Gus told me about your money problems, and your mother's illness . . . Ashley sweetheart, why in God's name didn't you tell me?'

'Well, at the beginning I was too proud,' she gave a little laugh, 'and later . . . I don't know . . . it never seemed to be the right moment. I was going to tell you at the party, and explain about my clothes.'

'My next question,' he broke in, 'how on earth do you manage to dress like that on no money?'

'It's Auntie Con,' she explained. 'She used to be a dressmaker. She could make a *Vogue* model out of an old flour sack.'

'I've met her. She gave me a cup of tea while I poured out my tale of woe . . . then she directed me to this place, on the understanding that I'd bring you back for lunch when I'd persuaded you to marry me.'

'That sounds like Auntie Con,' she laughed, 'and it sounds as if she liked you. Not that I ever imagined she wouldn't.'

'It's mutual,' he said. He checked his watch. 'If we don't get back soon, my sweet,' he remarked, 'your aunt will have finished making your wedding dress!'

He took up the peridot bracelet and fastened it on her wrist, then gently turning her hand over, he kissed the delicate blue veins that traced her white skin. 'Come, my darling,' he said, picking up the basket of primroses, 'let's go and tell them our news.'

Ashley nodded, too full of emotion to speak. For she knew now that she would be secure and blessed in the years to come. Their love would be a shield against the insecurities of the profession they were part of. And no matter what the future offered, life with Lucas would be a true and lasting partnership.

Coming Next Month in Harlequin Romance!

2641 NEW DISCOVERY   Jessica Ayre
A budding novelist hardly knows what to think when her
sophisticated publisher pays special attention to her. But when she
discovers he's married, she thinks the worst!

2642 CONNOISSEUR'S CHOICE   Dixie McKeone
A wealthy businessman ignites a young woman's anger and
underlying jealousy when he walks into her life with destructive
criticism on his lips and a rich and beautiful woman on his arm.

2643 COME INTO THE SUN   Barbara McMahon
The romantic West Indies is the scene for this intriguing story of a
young woman trying desperately to outrun her past. Just as love
catches up to her, so does her reputation.

2644 THE DREAMING DUNES   Valerie Parv
An Australian teacher cannot separate reality from fantasy in the
confusing world of cinema. She falls in love with a complicated
director who desires her one minute, rejects her the next.

2645 SEASON OF FORGETFULNESS   Essie Summers
Love triumphs in a most memorable manner when a young woman,
disillusioned by her fiancé, winds up working for a man who
dismissed his previous secretary for ruining his engagement.

2646 CARVER'S BRIDE   Nicola West
A mysterious sculptor refuses to settle for just any model to pose for
his latest commission. He contracts to hire one model in particular —
the woman who jilted him five years earlier.

ANNE WEALE
SUMMER'S AWAKENING

Anne Weale, bestselling
author of FLORA and
ANTIGUA KISS, has written her most sensitive and romantic
novel ever — SUMMER'S AWAKENING.

A lifelong battle with her weight kept Summer Roberts insecure
and isolated, yet inside she was warm, passionate and desperate
for love. Computer tycoon James Gardiner's entry into her
sheltered world was devastating in more ways than one — through
his kindness and unintentional
cruelty she emerged a slender,
beautiful woman, sure of herself
and sure of her love....

Watch for **Summer's
Awakening** at your favorite
bookstore in August, or send
your name, address and zip
or postal code, along with a
check or money order for
$4.25 (includes 75¢ for
postage and handling)
payable to Harlequin
Reader Service, to:

Harlequin Reader Service

In the U.S.
P.O. Box 52040
Phoenix, AZ 85072-2040

In Canada
P.O. Box 2800,
Postal Station "A"
5170 Yonge Street
Willowdale, Ontario
M2N 5T5

FA-1

Harlequin Stationery Offer

Personalized Rainbow Memo Pads for you or a friend

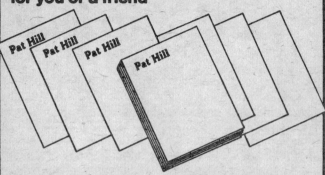

Picture your name in bold type at the top of these attractive rainbow memo pads. Each 4¼" x 5½" pad contains 150 rainbow sheets—yellow, pink, gold, blue, buff and white—enough to last you through months of memos. Handy to have at home or office.

Just clip out three proofs of purchase (coupon below) from an August or September release of Harlequin Romance, Harlequin Presents, Harlequin Superromance, Harlequin American Romance, Harlequin Temptation or Harlequin Intrigue and add $4.95 (includes shipping and handling), and we'll send you *two* of these attractive memo pads imprinted with your name.

- -

Harlequin Stationery Offer

(PROOF OF PURCHASE)

NAME_____

(Please Print)

ADDRESS_____

CITY_____ STATE_____ ZIP_____

NAME ON STATIONERY_____

Mail 3 proofs of purchase, plus check or money order for $4.95 payable to:	Harlequin Books P.O. Box 52020 Phoenix, AZ 85072	1-3

Offer expires December 31, 1984. (Not available in Canada)   STAT-1

Introducing

Harlequin Intrigue

Because romance can be quite an adventure.

Available in August wherever paperbacks are sold.

INT-3

Watch for the Harlequin Intrigue Sweepstakes.
You could win a romantic Cunard Cruise for two!

No purchase necessary. Void where prohibited by law.